ELK FOR SALE

A Mystery Novel

by

Annis Oetinger

Some of the locations in this book are real while some are imaginary. The characters are all fictitious.

Another Brant Grayson Book by this Author
Snow Job

ISBN 0-9634757-2-X

Published by Sunriver Writers Group
Sunriver, Oregon

Printed by Maverick Publications, Inc.
Bend, Oregon

Dedication

To Bill for his encouragement and love

Acknowledgements

My thanks go to the many people who have patiently answered my questions. Sheriff Greg Brown of the Deschutes County Sheriff's Department started me on correct police procedures and kept me pointed in the right direction. Senior Troopers Scott Moore and Darrell Duggins of the Oregon State Police Game Enforcement Division let me accompany them on their patrols and gave me good ideas for plot twists. Ken Goddard, Director of the U.S. Fish and Wildlife Forensic Laboratory, showed me the impressive facility dedicated to curbing the trade in illegal wildlife.

There are numerous others – doctor, nurse, stable hand, gun dealer, auto salesman – who helped with information to make the story accurate. I'm grateful to all of them for their kindness. Any mistakes are mine, not theirs.

Foreword

With over thirty years in the field of fish/wildlife management, I have witnessed an assortment of wildlife violations ranging from an over-limit of trout to importation of illegally taken polar bear hides from Alaska. The poaching of our wildlife resources is all too prevalent.

On a visit to Yellowstone National Park a few years ago, I, along with several dozen tourists, watched a monstrous bull elk herd his harem from one end of the meadow to the other obviously feeling threatened by us. His rack of antlers would have made the top ten Boone and Crockett record book. For thousands of tourists, their only chance to see magnificent animals like this has been in our Park and Refuge systems where, in the last few years, poaching has increased considerably.

A year later, I read that this trophy elk was found by park rangers shot and left to rot except for his huge rack. The killer was traced and arrested. The tools to investigate these crimes are as sophisticated today as those of any other crime. Poachers can no longer feel safe from prosecution.

Unfortunately, more arrests and stiffer sentences have not deterred poachers from destroying many North American trophy game animals. On a world-wide scale it is increasing at an alarming rate. What a shame, for me, you and all generations to come.

Frederic Vincent – U.S. Fish and Wildlife Service, retired

Elk For Sale

Cast of Main Characters

Brant Grayson, a retired detective

Lisl Morley, convention manager for Rivermount Resort

Caro and Jud Weston, Doc and Angie Michaels and Elaine and Phil Campbell, friends of Brant and Lisl

Amber, Campbell's golden retriever

Lt. Hardin Metcalf, detective with Les Rapides County Sheriff's Department

Chuck Harrison, deputy sheriff

Tony Marcus, Trooper with Oregon State Police Game Enforcement Department

Colman Lewis, export-import dealer

Frank, owner of Frank's Bar in Lakeside

Barney Valent, Brant's contact at Frank's Bar

CHAPTER ONE

Late April

"And there you have it," Brant Grayson said as the hikers rounded the last bend on the trail. "I promised you a fantastic view to go with your picnic, and here it is."

"It's gorgeous," breathed Lisl Morley with enough enthusiasm to make Brant's day. Her green eyes sparkled with the light from the sky. "You knew just the right place." The other six hikers didn't have to take a vote to agree.

It was spectacular. The eight friends had hiked about four miles on a gentle upgrade to a wide shelf on a slope overlooking a meadow and lake with the Cascade Mountains of central Oregon rising behind. Mt. Bachelor, the popular ski area, sat directly in front of them shining white from the winter snows. The Three Sisters, a jumble of peaks from this angle, were next north with Broken Top a jagged heap in front and the sharp point of Mt. Jefferson poking up behind. Pine forests stretched from the far edge of the meadow to the foot of the mountains.

"This is perfect. I don't even mind that my feet wanted to stop about a mile back down the trail," Caro Weston said. She eased herself down onto a flat rock. "You long-legged types take only half as many steps as I do. We're always running to catch up, huh, Angie?"

Angie Michaels looked enough like Caro that they were used to people mixing them up. It was awhile after he met them before Brant could remember which was which. They'd been friends since high school, both with short curly hair, now gray, five feet two, and Caro with the blue eyes like the old song.

Their husbands, Jud Weston and Doc Michaels, were classmates in college. They'd met their wives there, and the foursome had been friends ever since.

"We're out of condition not hiking all winter," Angie said. "It's a good thing there are plenty of nice places to sit while we have our picnic." She sat down beside Caro, took her brown bag lunch from her day pack and laid out the contents – sandwich, apple, brownies, some trail mix and a can of juice.

Brant maneuvered around to sit next to Lisl on an old log while the others found suitable places. The late April sun warmed their backs as a cool breeze off the mountains fanned their faces. For a few minutes they were quiet with their mouths full of food.

Background music to go with lunch came from a brook fed by melting snow not far above them. The water burbled over rocks and moss, rushed down the slope and fanned out into the meadow before trickling into the lake. New grass showed through the brown left over from last season. No wildflowers poked up yet. It would be another month before the lupine, Indian paint brush, daisies and a host of other blossoms added color to the green.

Phil and Elaine Campbell had brought their golden retriever, Amber, with them. She happily plopped herself into the water. It never seemed to bother her that the temperature might be just a couple of degrees above freezing. Hikes with the Rivermount group were one of the joys of her canine life.

"Now, Phil," Elaine warned her husband, "don't let Amber shake all over everyone when she gets out of the water."

At the sound of her name, Amber came bounding over to see what food might be shared with her.

"Go on, mutt," Phil waved her away. "Take your wet fur somewhere else."

She loped off down the hill toward a thicket of pines on the edge of the meadow directly below.

Lisl took her eyes off the view and turned toward Brant. He noted with approval the way the auburn highlights in her dark hair glinted in the sun.

"This is just so beautiful," she told him. "The lake shining, the meadow just turning green and the mountains still so white. It's picture postcard perfect. So peaceful and quiet."

Abruptly Amber shattered the quiet with her barking. She came out of the thicket dragging a long stick.

"Drop that," Phil ordered, "and come up here. Behave yourself."

Amber came to join them, but something bothered here. Brant reached to scratch her ears. Usually she blissfully accepted such attentions, but this time she ignored him. Her paws worked up and down nervously, and she nudged Phil.

"I think Amber is trying to tell you something," Brant said. "She's sure bothered about it, whatever it is."

"Okay, I guess I've finished enough of my lunch," Phil told her as he stuffed the remains in his day pack. "What do you want to show me?" and he followed the dog down the slope. She ran on ahead and grabbed the stick again.

"Bring it here," Phil said. She came and laid it at his feet.

"Uh-oh, guys," he called to the others. "This isn't a stick, it's a leg bone from an elk." Amber's tail fanned the air in excitement as she headed for the thicket again.

"I thought I caught a whiff of something not too good," Angie sniffed. "Do you smell it too?"

"Now that you mention it, yes," Caro agreed, "and it's not just wet fur. Smells like something spoiled."

"Maybe we better go see what it's all about," Brant said. "Amber's sure revved up over it." He stowed his lunch trash, unfolded his long, lean frame and started down the hill with Doc and Jud right behind him. Elaine asked the women if they wanted to see what it's about.

"I'm not sure I do from the smell of it, but maybe we can stay upwind, and I'm curious what Amber has found," Lisl said. They picked their way down over the rocks and moss.

"Be careful," Angie cautioned. "It's kind of squishy here at the bottom."

Barking wildly, Amber wriggled her way into the tangle of dead branches and small trees. What the hikers saw as they pushed through behind the dog was enough to make anyone horrified, furious and sick all at once.

"Ugh, how awful," Lisl exclaimed. "It looks like a slaughterhouse gone berserk. Who would do such a terrible thing?"

A tangle of headless and partially butchered carcasses from at least three – maybe four – elk lay scattered under the dead pine branches and remnants of winter snow.

"Come here, Amber," Phil called. The dog was in a frenzy of agitation. She came to sit by him whining softly.

"Somebody killed these out of season," Phil said as he examined the nearest carcass. His dark eyes flamed with anger. He'd been retired only about a year from the U. S. Fish and Wildlife Service, and it wasn't the first time he'd seen sights like this.

"They must have been killed late in the year just before we had that big freeze, and they've been lying here frozen solid buried under the snow all winter. The coyotes have been at the kill and scattered it some – maybe last year, maybe this spring. We need to get the local Fish and Wildlife people out here to see if they can find any clues."

Slowly the group began to edge their way back out of the thicket. Brant was the last to leave. A spot of color caught his eye. He bent over and lifted the branches near him.

"Dead elk aren't the only things here. This is a man on top of one of the elk, and he's been shot in the back of the head."

CHAPTER TWO

Later the Same Day

Clouds moved across the sun, and a chill wind whistled through the tall ponderosa pines. Brant heard the various reactions to his find. Oh no, How awful! You're sure? You can't mean it. Who is it? Was it an accident? I think I'm going to be sick.

"I don't have any answers yet," Brant said as he backed out of the thicket. He looked at the seven faces turned toward him. Lisl's eyes glistened with unshed tears, and her lips were pressed tightly together. Caro had her hand over her mouth in an unconscious reflex against nausea. She'd be likely to cry over a dead chipmunk. Multiple dead elk and a murdered man were too much to absorb. She turned to Jud who reached out an arm to comfort her. Angie's face reflected anger and disgust – anger at unnecessary violence and disgust with people who did it. She'd been a nurse, and the results of violence weren't new to her.

Elaine, along with Phil, had seen animal kills before. She felt contempt for the killers and sorrow for the animals uselessly slaughtered. Phil met Brant's gaze with a "let's get busy" look as his eyes roved over the scene already searching for clues. Doc's automatic reflexes also kicked in. He'd worked in the medical examiner's office when he was going to med school, and his knowledge had been a big help on the murders the group had encountered on their ski trip last winter.

"Jud," Brant suggested, "how about if you take the women and hike out as fast as you can to a phone. Call the sheriff's office and talk to Hardin Metcalf. He'll know who else to call. Tell him what we've found and that I'll wait here for him. If he isn't around, ask for Chuck Harrison. Okay?"

"Sure," Jud answered. "I guess you don't need all of us here. If there's any message, I'll come back. Come on, ladies." He tried to sound capable in spite of the uneasy feeling in his stomach.

"Brant, we can't just go off and leave you here with this – this horror," Caro said as she waved her hand toward the trees. A tear edged down her cheek.

"No, come on, Caro," Jud urged her. "Brant and Doc and Phil can take care of things. It's awful, but we can't be any help here. Better we should go call the cops as fast as we can."

"I'll take Amber," Elaine said. "You don't need her romping around over everything. She's done her part finding this mess. Let's go find the car, Amber." The dog raced back up the slope and headed along the trail.

Lisl put her hand on Brant's arm and searched his angular face. Her expression showed a mixture of horror and concern. "You're sure it wasn't an accident?"

"I'm only sure it wasn't a suicide. Shot by his fellow poachers accidentally or on purpose, I don't know."

"And you plan to find out." A frown creased her forehead.

He smiled reassuringly. "Don't worry. When Hardin gets here, he can take over, and I'll be out of it."

"That's what you said last winter, and look what happened. You were nearly killed. I wish you'd manage to stay retired." Her forehead had worry lines as she moved to follow the other women up the slope. Brant felt a moment of pleasure that she was concerned for his welfare. He watched her neatly arranged five feet six figure as she climbed the hill, then turned reluctantly back to the business of murder and poaching.

Part way up the slope Lisl looked back at the men below. Brant's sandy colored hair shone almost white against the dark trees. He huddled with Doc and Phil as they discussed their plans. Lisl had met Brant just last winter, and her feelings about him were ambivalent. She enjoyed his company more than anyone else she'd met in recent years. But a policeman? A retired detective who couldn't seem to stay retired? During the investigation last winter on the ski trip, it had been fun and informative to help him in the beginning. But when the murderer closed in on Brant and tried to kill him, the fun turned to pure fear. Lisl shook her head as she went on up the hill. She wasn't sure how much fear she could stand along with the fun.

Jud led the way following Amber. They turned back toward the trailhead where the cars were parked. He set a brisk pace and hoped the women could keep up. His white hair, which had once been black to match his eyes, led like a flag down the trail.

He wondered where the nearest telephone would be. Too bad they hadn't brought a cellular one, but who would think they'd be needing a phone on a pleasant little hike. In the summer there were business places open that catered to the tourists, but it was too early in the season for them. He hadn't paid much attention as they drove up to the Forest Service parking lot at the trailhead. He might have to go all the way to the highway.

He knew why Brant preferred to have Hardin Metcalf come out. Even though Brant was retired now as a detective, he and Hardin had established a good working relationship in dealing with the murders on their ski trip to Indian Lake last January. As Jud's mind raced ahead, he could hear his wife fretting behind him, but he didn't bother to listen.

"What a dreadful way to end such a beautiful day. Who could have done it, and who is the man Brant found?"

"Maybe he was someone who just happened by. Could it be like that?" Elaine asked.

"Who could possibly kill those beautiful animals and then just leave them there? Such a cruel and senseless thing to do," Lisl lamented.

"Trophy heads are worth a good bit of money, I've heard," ever-practical Angie said, "although I can't imagine who would want to pay money for a dead animal head to hang on the wall, especially when you didn't shoot it yourself. That's kind of cheating, really tacky."

Those heads are big and heavy, plus the meat they took too," Elaine said "How did they carry it?"

"But the man Brant saw? What about him? What can that mean? Did he fall or get shot by the hunters by mistake? Ugh. It couldn't be another murder," and Lisl shuddered.

Jud reached the cars ahead of the women. He had the doors and back of his Blazer unlocked and Amber loaded in the rear by the time the others arrived.

"It'll be a little crowded with five of us and the dog, but we'll manage," he said.

They had come in two cars, and the men remaining behind would need the other one later. Jud wheeled the Blazer around as soon as his passengers were in and gunned down the forest road as fast as he felt was prudent.

"Anyone remember if we passed somewhere that would have a phone?" he asked.

"How about the Trout River Fish Hatchery?" Elaine suggested. "They should be open."

It was about fifteen miles to the fish hatchery. Jud couldn't think of a phone any closer. As he drove, his mind was a jumble of thoughts about what they'd found, about his friends and about what looked like another murder.

He'd never come close to a murder before their cross-country ski trip last winter, and now here it looked like they'd run into another. He hoped it wasn't going to become a steady part of his life. Brant was the only one in this group who had any experience in homicides. After all, he'd been a big city detective. Doc, in his medical practice, had certainly seen death and the results of violence, but that wasn't quite the same as figuring out who committed a murder.

Caro sat in the front seat beside Jud, but she squirmed around to be able to talk with the others in back.

"Elaine," she asked, "did Phil run into things like this often when he was working? Do people go around just killing wildlife like that?"

"All the time. Sometimes it's for food, but more often it's for money or just for the excitement. That was one of Phil's biggest jobs – trying to keep ahead of the poachers." Elaine's brown hair whirled as she shook her head in disgust.

"But if it's for food – if people are going hungry – why isn't it okay?" Lisl asked. "There are certainly scads of deer around. We see them all the time at home."

"How can you tell if it's for food or target practice? You can't just let anyone shoot a deer or elk anytime."

"So you have to get a license, and go during the season. And how do they know how many licenses to give?" Angie asked.

"The various game departments get their data together and decide how many deer and elk or whatever they can allow to be killed and still not harm the herds," Elaine explained. "If it's been a good year with plenty of feed, they'll allot more hunting tags, but if it was a bad winter or too dry a summer and lots of animals died, then there won't be as many tags."

"It's so sad and so dreadful," Caro mourned. "I have a big lump in my stomach just thinking about it all, all of it, the elk and especially that poor man."

It had taken them nearly an hour to hike out and another twenty minutes or so on the winding mountain roads to get to the hatchery. Jud drove in, parked and headed for the office.

"Hi, I'm Jud Weston," he introduced himself to the man behind the desk. "Do you have a phone I can use to call the sheriff's office in Farwell?"

"Sure," the workman said. "You got a problem?"

"Yes, we've stumbled on a bunch of dead elk and a dead person too, up by the lakes."

"No kidding!" The man looked surprised. "Come on this way. I'll ring for you."

Jud followed the workman into the back room.

"Hi, this is Mel at the fish hatchery. I have someone here with a problem, needs to talk to you. Here," and he handed the phone to Jud.

"This is Jud Weston. May I speak to Hardin Metcalf, please?"

"I'm sorry, Lt. Metcalf is out of the office. Can someone else help you?"

"How about Chuck Harrison?"

"Deputy Harrison is with Lt. Metcalf. What seems to be the problem?"

"A group of us were on a hike today, and we found a mess of dead elk and a person's body too. Do you know Brant Grayson?"

"Yes, I know Brant."

"Well, he's with us, and he said to call Hardin or Chuck, and he'll wait where we found the mess. Is there any way you can reach Hardin?"

"Yes, it happens he's south of town already and should be available very soon. Where shall I tell him to come?"

"Tell him I'll wait for him at the Trout River Fish Hatchery and point him in the right direction."

"He should be there within a half hour."

Jud went back out to the car to report that Hardin and Chuck would be there in about half an hour, they'd give them instructions about where to find the three men, and then go home and wait to see what came of it all.

"Let's get out and look at the fish," Caro suggested. It's better than just sitting in the car. I don't even want to think about what we found."

Jud and the four women wandered around looking in the various tanks at thousands of squirming, darting fish ready to stock the mountain lakes for the summer season. Clouds by now covered the sky while the wind rushed through the pines and rustled the grass.

"How did it get so cold so suddenly?" Lisl asked.

In less than half an hour the sheriff's department car wheeled into the hatchery parking lot. Hardin and Chuck greeted their friends from last winter.

"So where are the guys and the elk?"

Jud told him where the group had been hiking.

"Okay," Hardin said. "I know where you mean. Sorry to rush off, but we'd better be on our way. Thanks for the call, and we'll see you later."

Hardin turned into the trailhead parking area, heaved his big frame out of the car and started up the trail. Chuck hurried after him. The sun headed down toward the west by the time they reached the ledge.

"Brant," he called. "We're coming down."

"Good," Brant yelled from among the trees. "Just follow your nose."

He's right, Hardin muttered to himself. Smells kind of ripe.

Brant had been busy off and on during the winter helping at the county sheriff's office with the investigation of the ski trip murders. At first he'd been reluctant to get involved in police work after his retirement, but he found it wasn't so bad. Kind of nice, really. He could work when he was needed, but there wasn't the pressure of the big city department he'd left behind.

Hardin hastened down the slope and pushed his way into the thicket of trees and brush.

"Oh, shit!" he exclaimed when he saw the carnage. "Why do we have jerks in the world who'd do something like this. What d'ya have so far?" he asked Brant.

"We've kept away from anything that looked critical. Some of it's easy to see. The heads have been hacked off and the best of the meat. Probably three or maybe four animals. Looks like people on horseback drove them toward this trap and then mowed 'em down. I'm not sure how many horses there were. At least two or three. The tracks were frozen, but they're filling with water now as things thaw out. The evidence won't last long if this warm weather keeps up."

"You're right," Hardin agreed. "I'll call the OSP game people and Fish and Wildlife when we get back to town. Get 'em up here as soon as possible. We'll come back tomorrow and make casts of some of the tracks and take pictures of everything. So what about the body?"

Brant slipped easily back into his detective mode. When he was with his friends at leisure, his craggy face looked gentle, and his eyes were almost-blue with smile lines creasing his cheeks. His work face turned stern, and his eyes changed to a no-nonsense gray under his thatch of sandy hair. He gave Hardin a succinct report.

"It's a man. The bones are partially scattered like the elk. Predators, probably coyotes, have been messing around. Maybe even a bear."

Brant lifted the dead branches hiding the body. "He's wearing a corduroy jacket, an old plaid flannel shirt and well-worn khaki pants. The boots are heavy-duty but beat up. I doubt if the clothes will tell us much. Too generic. He had them a long time, or they came from a thrift shop. Lying here under the snow all winter hasn't improved them any, but I doubt they were clean when he started out."

"Do you know yet what happened to him?"

"Yes, we found his head with a bullet hole in the back and his face blasted off. His buddies could have shot him by mistake, but it looks more like they decided he wasn't useful to them anymore."

"Could be," Hardin agreed.

"His clothes held most of the body together. Whoever did it wanted to hide what happened as long as possible with these dead branches. They were lucky the snow came so soon after they did their dirty work."

"And maybe it will be lucky for us that everything froze so quickly. Here, help me put up the crime scene tape. We'll rope off the whole area. I guess you can be the guardian, Chuck. We'll send a relief out for you later, and then we'll get a crew out tomorrow so we'll have the whole day to sift everything."

Phil wandered out toward the meadow while Brant and Doc helped Hardin and Chuck wrap the yellow tape around the thicket of trees.

"Bring it clear out here," he called to them. "There are lots of tracks that'll be important. Look here."

The others joined him. A lumpy morass of tracks scarred the meadow grass with prints of elk overridden by horseshoes. The spring grass hadn't yet grown enough to obliterate the signs.

"There were probably three, maybe four horses," Phil said, "and one of them has a distinctive shoe. See this little extra indent? You can find that print a number of places. If we follow back across the meadow far enough, there'll be some place where we'll be able to tell how many horses and where they unloaded and loaded up again and what kid of cars and trailers and all that stuff."

Hardin sighed. "This looks like one that'll keep us busy for awhile, us and a lot of other people. I'll pick you up about 8:30 in the morning," he said to Brant. "Bring your lunch. We may be here awhile. You other guys can come too if you want."

CHAPTER THREE

Next Day

Phil and Brant were waiting for Hardin when he stopped by next morning.

"Doc couldn't come," Brant explained, "but Phil thought he might be some help tracking. He's had lots of experience in that."

"Glad you could come," Hardin said. "My crime scene people have gone on ahead in a pick-up. We'll meet them there. I called the game people at the State Police yesterday, told 'em what's here, and they sent a man out to relieve Chuck. They'll be out in force today, too."

"Looks like the guys have hiked on in," Hardin commented as he drove into the Forest Service parking lot at the lakes trailhead. "I told 'em to leave some of the gear for us to pack in. I'll see what we have," as he inspected the sheriff's department pick-up already parked there alongside Oregon State Police cars and pick-ups.

"Morris'll be hard at his photo-ops by the time we get there. Police photographers don't come any better. Here, you take this pack, and you this one," as he handed them to Brant and Phil and then shouldered another. "Investigations out in the wilds aren't exactly like being in the heart of downtown."

Hardin was a big man, taller even than either Brant or Phil, and outweighed them by more than a few pounds. First glance might have given the impression he was overweight, but every pound was solid as a rock. He set a brisk pace up the trail, and they reached the ledge in under an hour.

"Yo, Morris, Jim," Hardin called. "We're coming down."

The early spring sun of yesterday was hidden in gray clouds, and the temperature had returned to winter. Ice edged the little creek, and frost rimed the grass and trees. It was almost too cold to work, but it had the advantage of deadening the smell of decay.

Hardin introduced Morris Stein and Jim Jerrold. Morris acknowledged the newcomers without taking his eye away from his cameras. He was short and round but moved with surprising agility and great care as he snapped picture after picture. Starting from the outer boundary of the yellow tape marking the scene he gradually moved into close-ups of the elk carcasses and the man's body.

"Anything interesting so far?" Hardin asked.

"We haven't been here long – just a few minutes," Jim told him. He was the tall and thin one of the pair with a face that made Brant immediately think of a hawk. Same eyes and nose with hair that looked like ruffled feathers.

Hardin introduced the supervisor of the Oregon State Police group, Bert Horgan.

"You know all the guys," Bert said to Hardin. He turned to Brant and Phil to introduce Tony Marcus, a dark-haired, six foot trooper with a crooked smile. "He's from our game enforcement department and is our expert tracker. From what Hardin told me last night, I figured a good tracker would be useful. The other guys are George, Henry, Weldon and Ward." He waved his arm at four other men from the State Police and the Fish and Wildlife department, already hard at work around the area. "I brought a full crew, crime lab, etc." he said.

"Turned up anything yet?"

"Routine so far," Bert answered. "Plenty of clues around thanks to having everything frozen all winter. It's a case of getting all we can find now before it thaws too much. I know Morris and Jim will be a big help."

Phil turned to Tony. "Mind if I come along with you?"

"Glad to have you. You were here yesterday. What did you find?"

"Plenty. Now that it's frozen again this morning, I think it'll be like an open book. You the plaster cast man?" he asked Jim.

"Yep."

"I found some hoof prints yesterday that looked interesting. It was out here." He and Tony headed toward the meadow side of the thicket with Jim bringing his gear.

"There, this one," Phil pointed. "See that funny little notch in one shoe. I found it in other places, but this one is as clear as any. And then there are some for a horse that was big – bigger shoes than usual and deeper prints. Where the ground was dry, the tracks haven't lasted, but enough of them were in the boggy areas that we can see where they came from and where they went out. I'll just follow along with Tony and see what we find," and the two men headed into the fog around the lake.

Brant and Hardin left Morris to his photographs while they conferred with the State Police and Fish and Wildlife people who had begun a systematic inspection of the site. They started at the outer edge on the meadow side where Jim was taking casts of the hoof prints.

"Here are cartridge casings right by the boot prints." Brant bent to check the casings and the footprints. Hardin carefully put the casings in an evidence bag after Morris had photographed their location.

"I'm thinking," Brant said as he watched Hardin and Morris, "Those casings aren't quite where I'd expect for a right-handed person. Was he shooting left-handed maybe? Not too many people shoot left-handed even if they actually are left-handed. Something to think about."

"Yeah, I'll make a note of that."

"These footprints and hoof prints have held their shape amazingly well over the winter. The snow packed down on them, but it's still easy to see the shapes. One of them was wearing cowboy boots, and one had work boots something like a logger might wear, not new but in good condition. The other looks very worn. It's the one that heads on into the middle. Matches the boots on our body over there. He and the logger's boot must have been cutting the heads and meat and bringing them back to the cowboy boots who was loading them on the horses."

The morning wore on as the men worked over the area taking photos, casts, samples of dirt, tissue samples, blood, hair, hides or whatever else might yield a clue. Phil and Tony were out of sight across the meadow. Fog hid the mountains, hung over the lake and drifted around the trees.

After Morris had taken all the pictures he wanted of the man's remains, Hardin brought the body bag. He and Brant eased the corpse in, trying to keep it as much intact as possible.

"We'll get fingerprints right away before he thaws out," Hardin muttered.

Phil called to them from part way out in the meadow.

"Hey, bring the camera and other stuff out here. We've found something interesting."

Everyone headed out to where he stood.

"What you got?" Hardin asked.

"These cartridge casings are for crackers – noisemakers. Those things aren't all that easy to come by. You have to have a fire marshall's permit. Somebody went to a little extra trouble on this operation to be sure the elk went toward what turned out to be a natural trap."

"So we make a note of them, where we found them, put them in a bag. One more little piece that just may help. You got your picture, Morris?"

The men headed back toward the thicket.

"Did anybody stop for lunch?" Phil asked.

"Didn't get around to it. We were having too much fun," Hardin answered drily.

"How much more you got to do?"

"Don't know. How about it, Morris? Jim?"

"'bout finished," Morris said. "Not much I've missed."

"I can quit anytime," Jim told them. "The lab'll be busy enough with all this. Damn poachers. Whyn't they get a job to make some money instead of doin' this?"

"You find anything else interesting?" Brant asked Phil.

"Yeah, they might as well have left us a note saying what they were doing." Phil's bony face, weathered from a lifetime outdoors, broke into a grin. "The tracks aren't hard to read. There were three of them and four horses. Since they left one rider behind here, they probably loaded both his horse and the extra horse with the loot. Parked out on a logging road with the horse trailer. They had a dual wheel pick-up to haul the big trailer. Not much sign of any other traffic either before or since."

"You've found out a lot already. Good going. It'll help," Hardin said "You ready to pack it up here, Bert?'

"Won't be much longer. Go on out, and we'll be right behind you."

"Okay. We're going to have a full load to carry with all this gear and the body bag too.

CHAPTER FOUR

That Evening

The phone rang.

"Rivermount Lodge Convention Center. May I help you?" Lisl asked.

"I'd like to arrange a convention for five hundred people for the Fourth of July weekend."

Lisl rolled her eyes. What kind of idiot thought he could arrange a convention in April for the busiest weekend of the summer for 10 people , let alone 500?

"I'm sorry, sir, but that weekend is fully booked. Perhaps -," a soft chuckle interrupted her.

"Oh, Brant, you toad." She recognized his voice. "What do you think you're doing, giving me a heart attack?"

"Just wanted to see how you handle the not-too-bright public. More important, wanted to see if you'd like to go out to dinner with me."

"I'd love to, but why don't you come over to my house for a change? I took a casserole out of the freezer at noon, and there's plenty for two."

"That sounds even better. I'll bring a bottle of wine and some French bread. What time?"

"I was just about ready to leave. Give me half and hour, and we'll be in business."

"Come in," Lisl called when the doorbell rang. "You're right on time," she said as Brant came into the kitchen. "Everything is just ready for me to leave it to cook by itself while we sit down and relax."

"Smells terrific, and you look great too. I like that shirt."

It was a print in shades of green to match her eyes and complement the pink tinge on her cheekbones.

"Thank you," she said. "What do you have there?"

Brant set an armful of packages on the counter. "Here's the wine, bread, and I bought the last two slices of cheesecake at the bakery. Couldn't let them go to waste."

"How nice." Lisl's smile revealed a touch of mischief. "I love a man who is thrifty like that, and I love cheesecake too."

"Hey, I like your house," Brant said looking around. He'd been widowed shortly before he retired and moved to Rivermount. Last winter's ski trip had introduced him to Lisl, and they'd been dating occasionally since then. He'd picked her up at her house a number of times, but this was the first time he had been further inside than the front hall. "Nice view of the mountain and meadow."

Horses grazed in the distance and Mt. Bachelor stood out in silhouette against the pink evening sky.

"Thanks. I'm glad you like it. Fine for me. Big enough but not too much. I don't have time for housekeeping. Would you like to light the fire? Matches are on the hearth. And I'll pour us a drink."

As the flames crackled up around the juniper wood in the fireplace, Lisl brought a tray from the kitchen with two glasses of scotch and water and a dish of crisp crackers with a wedge of camembert cheese. She settled onto the sofa while Brant sank into the big chair.

"Isn't it nice to have the daylight lasting longer now?" Lisl said. "I love the snow, but I did get rather weary of the dark this winter. Now it seems like spring will really get here someday. So tell me what you did today. How did it go? What did you find out?"

Brant ran his hand through his hair that always looked like a sheaf of wheat. His steel-gray eyes closed for a minute.

"This beats going out for dinner somewhere. I can really relax here, and I feel like I need it," he sighed. "To answer your questions, it was hard work and a long day, but we made considerable progress. It'll take awhile to sift the evidence, but there're some things we know for sure. Coyotes had been at the kill and scattered the remains around, but we counted four elk killed, and there were four horses used. Phil and Tony from the State Police Game Department did a great job of tracking. One horse was bigger than average, one drags its feet, and one had a slight nick out of a shoe. The other was pretty standard issue."

"They could tell all that?"

"And more. They followed the tracks all the way across the meadow around the end of the lake to a small Forest Service road. Some of the tracks were messed up by now with the freeze and thaw, but enough of them are still clear. The truck the poachers used was a dual wheel pick-up, new tires. The dirt on the road was pretty hard last fall, but our men found a mushy spot with enough tracks to see where they unloaded the horses from the trailer. Then they spread out and moved across the meadow, one of them leading one horse. The elk were at the end of the lake, and they moved ahead of the horses toward where we found them. The poachers used crackers to help get the elk into the trees. They picked their place carefully. The natural terrain formed a trap in that thicket of trees with the hill behind."

"What do you mean, crackers?" Lisl asked. "Is that some kind of bait?"

"No, they're a special kind of shell that makes a noise like firecrackers but isn't a bullet. You have to get a permit from the fire marshall to get them, but it's not too hard. People use them to scare off animals where they're doing damage."

"I've never heard of that before. Very interesting. And what else did you find? Any idea who they were or who the dead man was?"

"It looks like there were three of them from the three different sets of boot tracks. One was leading the extra horse on the way in, and two were leading the other two going back since obviously one man didn't go out with them."

"But how can you tell someone was leading a horse?" Lisl asked.

"If the tracks for one horse follow another at a consistent distance apart all the way, it's a good bet the front one is leading the back one," Brant explained.

"Aha, I can understand that," Lisl agreed. "So who were they? Any ideas?"

"Nothing definite. I'm guessing the dead one may have been a transient recruited by the other two and disposed of when they didn't need him anymore. It seems unlikely he was shot by mistake when the shot was squarely through the back of the head."

"How awful! To just dispose of a person like an old coat." Lisl shook her head. "And what about the others?"

"No idea yet. Probably not affluent if they're making money this way. One of the guns was probably a bolt action 30.06, but the other may have been a 300 Winchester Magnum."

"What does that mean? I don't know anything about guns."

"The 30.06 is older style, cheaper, but the Winchester isn't cheap. These were people who were looking to make some extra money selling the heads for trophies. They didn't bother with anything but the choicest of the meat.

"Then how do they sell the stuff? Who buys that kind of thing? Would someone around here know where to market trophy heads?"

"And that's a good question. I expect the State Police game people know the pathways for sales. Maybe it's just by word of mouth. Obviously you can't go around advertising you have elk heads shot out of season and without a permit. I've never been involved much in this sort of thing."

"Is there big money in it?"

"Those four elk heads in the right market, assuming they were in good condition might bring anywhere from ten to twenty thousand dollars. Each."

Lisl's jaw dropped. "You must be joking! I can't believe it. That is mind boggling. So much."

"S'truth, so the game people tell me," Brant confirmed. "For other rare game like big horn sheep it can be in the six figures. It makes poaching attractive to people who don't mind breaking the law or destroying our wildlife."

"I'm totally amazed," Lisl said. She sat for a moment in stunned silence. Then she turned her head. "Let's shift the scene to the kitchen. The bread is in the oven, and the casserole smells done. It's a beef stew. I'll toss a salad, and then we'll be ready. Would you like to set the table? Everything is laid out there on the buffet."

Brant did as directed with the place mats and silverware. The table was a round one in an alcove surrounded with windows looking out on the forest which had faded into shadows in the twilight. He returned to the kitchen and opened the bottle of pinot noir.

"Smells wonderful and I'm really hungry. It was an active day, and we never got around to lunch."

"Everything is ready. Go ahead and pour the wine while I put things on the table."

By unspoken consent the conversation over dinner moved from the events of yesterday to subjects more suitable for mealtime. Golf, hiking, weather, new houses, the approaching vacation season with the usual hordes of tourists crowding the village.

"Would you like another helping?" Lisl asked.

Couldn't eat another bite," Brant told her. "That was really super. Sure beats my own cooking."

"Let's have our coffee and dessert in the living room."

"Good idea, and I'll make you an offer you can't resist. You put the leftovers away while I clean up the dishes. That'll give our dinner time to settle before we pack that cheesecake in on top of it."

"Oh, Brant, you don't have to clean up."

"I'm the best dishwasher-packer you ever met, so no argument, okay?"

Lisl smiled her agreement. Before she met Brant last winter, her social life had been less than exciting – mainly confined to events related to her job. Her occasional dates with Brant injected more fun in life. She liked his good-natured smile and easy-going personality. It didn't fit her image of a homicide detective, and she wondered what criminals might have thought when they faced him. Did they think Brant would be a pushover? They'd be surprised, she knew, after watching him handle the murders last winter.

As the dishwasher hummed into its cycle, they carried their dessert and coffee into the living room and relaxed in well-fed comfort.

"Are you going traveling anywhere this year?" Lisl asked.

"Hadn't really thought about it," Brant answered. "I guess I'll hang around here and see how this case progresses."

"What happens to the man you found?"

"We packed him out today. The body goes to the medical examiner's office in Portland. It'll be awhile before we get a report back. If his fingerprints are on file anywhere, we'll find out who he was, and maybe that'll point to who killed him." Brant sighed. "On the other hand, if he was a transient, even finding out who he was may not give us any idea who shot him."

"What if he doesn't have any fingerprints on file anywhere?"

"That'll make the job harder. But a surprising percentage of people have their fingerprints on file somewhere. From the looks of him, I'd say our best chance of luck may be if he's ever been in trouble with the law."

"And that's another thing I don't understand. How do you get a match on fingerprints when there may be thousands to look through. It could take forever."

"It used to be like that, and finding the right match was more luck than science. Now we have a new weapon against the bad guys which speeds the process immensely. It's called AFIS which stands for Automated Fingerprint Identification System. It's all done by computers – don't ask me how. It was really just getting up and running before I retired."

"That sounds fantastic. So much of the time it seems as if the bad guys are gaining on us. It's nice to hear about something that may help us. It looks like such a hopeless job with this case – so few clues about the man and since it happened so long ago. And if he's some tramp who just wandered into town, will the police work too hard trying to find out who killed him?"

"They'll work just as hard on his case as if it had been you or me. And there are more clues than you think. The fact that it happened months ago is a disadvantage, but having the freeze and snow come right on top of the crime is our good luck. The people who did it counted on having plenty of time go by before it was discovered. But they didn't count on clues being preserved so well."

"All this fascinates me. How can you know so much about what happened already?"

"All those branches on top of the mess didn't just fall there. They were put there to hide what happened from anyone hiking that trail late in the season. Another winter when the weather might have stayed mild much longer or the snow wasn't so deep that the predators couldn't get at the scene much – that would have been harder for us. And it was their bad luck that Amber was along. Any other hikers might have smelled something bad and figured it was just a dead animal and moved away from the smell."

"Well, I'll admit you and Phil and the others seem to have found out quite a bit," Lisl said.

"And we're only started. The state crime lab will be interested in the man, and the game division in the elk. Of course those things overlap. We have ballistics and boot and horseshoe prints and the man's clothes and the tire tracks of the vehicles they used. Lots of leads, and somewhere in the mess it will lead us to who did the killing and who paid them for it."

Brant leaned his head back in the chair and closed his eyes.

"You're tired."

"Yeah, long day outdoors in the not-so-fresh air up there. I should get home. I have a golf game tomorrow, and you have to go to work."

"Don't rush off. Relax awhile."

"That's too tempting. If I sit here longer, I might never get up."

"That'd be all right," Lisl smiled.

"No, I'd better go." Brant pushed himself out of the comforting depths of the chair and headed for the door. Lisl looked at him for a long moment before she stood up.

"Thanks for the super dinner and the chance to share my day with you. You're a good listener and questioner. You get my thoughts sorted out for me." Brant looked down into Lisl's upturned face and kissed her. He'd had no intention of doing that. It just seemed to happen of its own volition. Lisl's eyes widened in surprise for an instant, then her usual smile twinkled.

"Thanks. I needed that. Let's do it again sometime," she teased.

Brant had the dreadful feeling he was back in junior high wanting to date the most desirable girl in school. Something was going on here, and he felt totally out of touch, out of sync, out of his depth. So many years had gone by since he'd been in a serious dating mode.

"Uh, you're welcome, and sure thing. We'll get together again real soon. And thanks again." He reached for the doorknob with the unhappy notion that he was being less than suave. "I'll call you tomorrow," and he blundered toward his car.

Lisl closed the door quietly and leaned on it. Questions rippled through her mind. She knew Brant's wife had died. Was there something there that held him back? Lisl was sure he liked her. Otherwise they wouldn't have had this evening or any of their other dates. And the kiss? Was it just casual? A sudden impulse? She wasn't sure enough of her own feelings to begin to diagnose Brant's.

Lisl knew she'd become steadily more interested in Brant ever since they'd met last winter. Where were they headed? He'd been married and widowed. That couldn't help but mean he was carrying a large load of emotional baggage into any new relationship.

And then there was her own emotional baggage left over from her early marriage and divorce, with the years since, of dating and acquaintances she had never allowed to progress into anything meaningful.

Among various problems which led to her divorce had been her ex-husband's penchant for daring escapades – sky diving, hang-gliding, bungee-jumping, skiing uncharted terrain, driving race cars – you name it and he'd try it. She had spent too many hours waiting for him to appear where he was supposed to meet her – and too many times seeing him arrive on a stretcher. Too many trips to the emergency room with fright at what the diagnosis would be. It never occurred to him that such stress for his wife was a problem. That wasn't the only reason for the divorce, but she had no desire to live again on the edge of terror for someone she loved, and have that love die.

And therein lay the reason for her ambivalence about Brant. She liked him very much and knew he returned the feeling. If she allowed it, love might blossom. Since he was retired now from police work, where was the problem? Just that he'd come close to being killed by the murderer on the ski trip last winter, and now here he was in the middle of another case. She knew better than to believe him when he said he'd let Hardin take over. She could tell he was already hooked on the mystery, and anyway, even if he had the best intentions of staying out of it, Hardin would find a way to get him involved.

As she locked the doors and turned off the lights, Lisl decided she'd just wait and see. She didn't have to make any firm decision yet. Even though Brant was ten years older than she was, he really was so very attractive. I'll just wait and see what develops, she thought.

Heading home in the dark, quiet night, Brant's mind was kicking him all the way. You dummy, what'd you go and kiss her for, well why not, and she wasn't angry about it, she liked it, I think, and you've known her for three months now, long enough for a friendly kiss. Just a friendly one?

The face of his late wife, Ann, flashed into his mind, and she was smiling. Brant wanted to reach out to her, but she faded away to be replaced by Lisl. He and Ann had talked about his future as she was dying. She was too young to die, but that was beyond their power to change, and he was too young to live along the rest of his life. She hoped he would meet someone nice to share his remaining years. She'd left him a legacy of marital happiness to build on. Maybe Lisl was the one to fill that aching void in his life.

CHAPTER FIVE

Early May

Brant heard a voice call him as he walked by the Justice Center Building in Farwell. More than a week had passed since the Rivermount group's hike. He turned around. It was Lt. Metcalf.

"Hardin, hi. How's everything?"

"Thought you'd be out on the golf course."

Brant laughed and looked up at the sky where gray clouds scudded across an occasional blue patch. Periodically a shower drifted down.

"If it were late fall with winter coming soon, I might play on a day like this, but heading into summer, I can afford to wait for something better."

"Since you're here, come on in. Have you got a minute? Some of the lab reports have been coming in on your elk find."

"Sure. I've been wondering what you've found out." Brant followed Hardin up the walk and into his office.

They settled themselves with cups of coffee while Hardin rummaged through the papers on his desk looking for the right file.

"First, the man. About what we thought. The clothes led nowhere, probably second hand. He had holes in the socks which made an open blister on his heel, no underwear and dirt under his fingernails which were pretty ragged. Medical examiner says he was five feet ten. Fingerprints turned up a name – Jacob Kowalski – last known address a county jail in a small town in California for drunk and disorderly."

"Anything in the pockets?"

"Not much. A battered wallet with about ten dollars and a few pieces of change. So he wasn't entirely broke, but he wasn't rich. A match folder from Frank's Bar in Lakeside. We'll follow up on that. Try to find anyone who might remember him. Only thing of any real interest was a cracker shell in his jacket pocket. Looks like he was the one doing the noise making."

"Huh, maybe the other two didn't trust him with a real gun."

"You could be right about that. Ballistics have said there were casings from only two guns. I don't think we missed any with all of us looking. So it points to our deceased shooting crackers and the other two with the real thing."

"Okay, so much for that. What else?"

"You're impatient. What makes you think there is anything else?"

"Oh, just your sterling reputation for getting the facts," Brant chuckled.

"Well, you're right again. There is more. After counting the bones, it turned out to be four elk for sure, all bulls and one big and old. He must have had a great rack of antlers – a real king size trophy. That will bring a fat price. But there's more. We've found another three carcasses only a couple of miles away, not all in a bunch, but not far apart. Fisherman stumbled over 'em. And you'll be interested to know the casings are from the same guns. Oh, and I forgot. Found a couple of bullets still in the bodies. 300 Winchester Magnums. Somebody's got a real business going here."

"When were the other three shot?"

"Probably earlier. They were more decayed, and the coyotes had messed them around more. But the rest of the scene was the same as much as we could find. Foot prints and hoof prints weren't too good since the weather hadn't frozen yet. We could see what looked like the cowboy boots again, and the one extra big horse."

"You've been busy and very fruitfully so. The left-handed gun show up again?"

"Probably. The tracks weren't all that clear. As you recall, last fall was pretty dry until just before the snow came. But there's more," and Hardin chortled like a kid opening Christmas packages.

"More!"

"A bear this time. Skinned, paws taken, gall bladder taken. And best of all, same gun."

"Aha. Whoever's doing it is not just into elk, huh. That points to a bigger operation, I'd guess. We'd better get this thing solved before the wild animal population is decimated."

"Yeah, and I'm getting an idea. How would you like to go out tonight? Say to Frank's Bar. Have a few beers and chat up the locals."

"Why me?" Brant asked.

"Those folks down there are kind of clannish and more than a little suspicious of us. It's like pulling teeth for a lawman to get anything out of them. But they don't know you. They're really into hunting, and they just might say things to you that they wouldn't to us if you get started right. How about it?"

"Well, I suppose I could if you think it would work better." Brant's voice sounded dubious and less than enthusiastic, but Hardin chose to ignore that.

"Sure. Just get 'em going on hunting prospects and who shot the biggest whatever, and you'll be in."

CHAPTER SIX

Next Evening

The red neon light announcing Frank's Bar blinked on and off as Brant parked his car, thankful it was the usual nondescript, non-attention-getter vehicle he'd always favored. He'd chosen his clothes carefully, old hiking boots, khaki pants and a well-worn plaid flannel shirt that he kept for gardening chores.

He stepped inside the door and felt nearly pushed back out by the noise of raucous music and the haze of smoke. So few of his friends smoked anymore that he'd lost his tolerance for it.

The tavern was like a hundred or a thousand in small towns around the West. The once beautiful mahogany bar had suffered years of hard use. A mirror was pinned to the back wall by dusty glass shelves holding equally dusty glasses meant to serve more exotic drinks than the usual beer or whiskey. One end of the room held a motley collection of tables and chairs. An old juke box – no longer functioning – squatted at the other end with a mounted elk head staring down from the shadows above.

Eyes turned to see who had come in, and the room suddenly quieted. The music from the radio blared on in the background, but conversation came to a dead stop as everyone – customers and bartender alike – sized up the newcomer. Brant moved over to the bar.

"You Frank?" he asked. Brant looked the bartender over. He was built like a heavy duty truck. The dim light shone off his totally bald head sitting squarely on his shoulders with no apparent neck.

"Yeah. I'm Frank. What'll ya have?"

"Gimme a Bud," Brant ordered and plunked some money down.

"Yeah, sure," Frank said as he set a bottle on the bar, swept up the money and laid out the change. "You new around here?"

Brant took a long drink of the beer before answering. "Been around the area a few days. Looks pretty good. Think I might stay awhile. Heard there was good hunting in the fall. Maybe get some kind of job until then. When winter comes, I'll head on south."

The noise of conversation resumed. Brant took another drink and looked around. There were probably a dozen men in the bar, all dressed much like he was. They ranged in age from one who didn't look old enough to be in a bar up to a grizzled codger with only one eye, few teeth and a scruffy beard. Most except the youngest had already acquired pot bellies that overhung their belts or poked out between suspenders.

A tall, heavy fellow with rusty black hair detached himself from the group and wandered over to Brant. "Where ya from, stranger?"

He seemed to have been designated to find out more about the newcomer.

"Most anywhere. You name it, I been there. Been down in Nevada lately. Lots of different ways down there to pick up some money, but it began to get a little hot. Figured it was time to move on."

"Hot, huh. Weather or otherwise?"

"Whatever." Brant shrugged, drank some more beer and looked away. Let them put any interpretation on his answer they liked. It told them they could get just so nosy and no more.

"What kinda work ya looking for?"

"Whatta ya got around here besides loggin'? I hear that's down on accounta them environmentalists and some owl. I'm a good carpenter. Got any buildin' goin' on? Or fightin' forest fires. You're sure to need that 'fore the summer's over."

"Well now, there's some loggin' goin' on even with the damn owl thing, but mosta the crews are full. Lots of house buildin' up the road a piece at that fancy resort where all them rich Californians live. Some around here too. Forest fires are iffy – never know when they'll be needed beyond the regulars they hire for the whole season – the smoke jumpers and all those. You look kinda old for some of the heavy stuff."

Brant felt momentarily insulted. "I don't know about that. I'm still pretty fit, keep in shape, and at least I'm more dependable than some young kid who's all muscle includin' between the ears."

Everyone laughed at that except the underage specimen who tried to look offended.

"I'm outta beer," Brant said, "and I see you are too. Lemme buy ya another," and he signaled the bartender.

"Well now, that's nice of ya. I'm Barney Valent. Some of them's" and he waved his hand at the others, "my relatives. Lots of us Valents around these parts. So what's your name."

"Grady Brown," Brant said and shook hands. When using an assumed name he always tried to think of one not so far off his own that he'd forget to respond to it.

"So I might be able to put a job or two your way. Where ya stayin'?"

"In my car for now. I need a better place for a few months. You know of any? I'm not exactly broke, but don't want anything too fancy. Someplace where folks mind their own business."

"Hm. Lessee. You guys got any ideas?" and he turned to the rest of the room.

"How about where that Jake was?" said another man who looked like a close carbon copy of Barney.

"Yeah, don't look like he's ever comin' back. Went off and left all his gear last winter. He'd paid the rent ahead for awhile, but Maddy's been lookin' for a new roomer ever since the rent ran out. Not too bad a place if ya aren't fussy, private door, and Maddy'll fix ya meals now and then. I'll show ya where it is. But come on over and meet the rest of the guys."

Brant swung his long legs off the bar stool and ambled over to be introduced to an assortent of names, Harry, Ken, Will, Junior.

"So ya like huntin'?" Barney took the lead in the conversation. "What ya after?"

"Got elk and deer around here?" Brant asked

'Sure have. Either east or west for the elk. East is out in the flat, wheat and alfalfa. West is up in the meadows around the lakes. Plenty of deer too. Bear now and then."

"When's the elk season start around here?"

"Along in November or thereabouts. Depends on how particular you are about dates or permits."

"Uh huh. Get some good trophies?"

"Ya oughta see some of 'em," said one Brant remembered was named Kenny. "Spread out to here," and he held his arms as wide as they'd reach. "I got one myself last year traded to a guy for a good pick-up," and he sat back with a satisfied smile.

Other voices chimed in with tales of how big the racks of antlers were around here. Brant encouraged the stories with "no kidding" or "come on, now" at suitable points in the talk.

"You lookin' to hunt for yerself, or you plannin' to pick up a little money sellin' 'em?" Barney asked.

One of the other men spoke up. "Like Kenny says, you can get big money for those heads if you know where to sell 'em without getting' caught. I could use a few thousand bucks."

"That much, huh," Brant let his voice express interest. "If it's so big, how d'ya keep every Tom, Dick and Harry from cashin' in?"

Barney squinted his eyes through the smoke. "Well now, we pretty much know who b'longs here. Any those big city dudes come nosin' around with their fancy cars and cases of booze – they ain't likely to find any elk. Maybe somebody beat 'em to it, know what I mean?"

"But how about poachers?"

"We don't go much for poachers comin' in around here. They come once, they ain't likely to come again. Might get a bullet in their butt. Kinda like to keep things for the home folks. Don't want anybody stirrin' up the game people to pokin' around or any deputies."

"You sound like my kinda guys. Take care of your friends first," Brant agreed.

The old man with one eye spoke. "I think that Jake what was around here last year – I think he mighta been doin' somethin' like that. He had a wad of money one time when he was in here and was talkin' big and mysterious about where he got it. And didja ever think maybe he didn't take off and go south. Maybe somebody didn't like him talkin' so much. Know what I mean?"

"Hey, yeah," another of the group said. I just remembered. In the paper th'other day about those folks findin' them elk with their heads hacked off. Said there was a man found dead too. Said it likely was last winter and they could have been frozen under the snow until now. "S'pose it could have been that Jake? That's about when he been gone."

"Could be, uh huh, could just be," Barney said. "Just goes to show it don't pay to talk too much. Keep your mouth shut and ya ain't so likely to put your foot in it." Brant looked around the faces and saw some of the men shrink back into their chairs.

"Well, reckon I better be getting' on my way to someplace to hang my hat," Brant said. "Nice to meet all you guys. I'll see ya around."

"Hey, hold up just a minute and I'll take ya over to Maddy's. It's a place for the night at least, and if ya don't like it, ya can move on tomorrow."

"Well, thanks, Barney. Sure nice of you. See ya," and he waved to the rest of the gang. "Nice place ya got here," he said to Frank on the way out.

Barney climbed into a battered pick-up and headed down a side road away from the highway with Brant following along trying to remember the various turns they were making. One last turn and Barney stopped in front of a two story house with all the architectural charm of an apple box. It had clearly seen better days and hadn't been anything special when it was new.

Barney stomped up on the wooden porch and banged on the front door. A woman's voice from inside the door asked who was there.

"Me, Maddy. Barney. Open up, dearie. I brought ya a new roomer."

Brant could hear a bolt slide across, and the flimsy door opened. The woman in the doorway was short, fat and ugly. One of life's losers, he thought. Her frowsy housecoat was as shapeless as she was. Unkempt gray hair shadowed her squinty eyes. Brant experienced grave misgivings about what any room in this landlady's house would be like. At all cost he planned to avoid sleeping there.

"This here's Grady Brown," Barney introduced Brant. "This's Maddy Perkins, Grady. Show him that room ya got, Maddy, the one that Jake guy had."

"Show 'im yourself. You know where it is. I ain't climbin' those stairs this hour of the night. Jake's stuff is still there. Haven't got around to cleanin' it out. Hang on, I'll get the key," and she shuffled toward what looked like the kitchen. In a moment she was back with an old-fashioned key, the kind Brant remembered his family had at the beach house when he was a kid.

"Okay, ya old bat," Barney told her without rancor as he took the key, "I'll do your job for ya. Come on, Grady, around this way," and he went around the corner of the house.

Rickety wooden steps led up to a door on the second floor. Barney led the way up, unlocked the door and turned on a light. It was a bare bulb in the middle of the ceiling and managed to light only the center of the room, leaving the corners in shadow.

"Whadda ya think?" Barney asked. "Think it'll be okay? It ain't much, but it's cheap and quiet."

Brant's mind churned trying to think of an excuse for not staying without blowing his cover.

"Seems like it might do, but I got to go on to Farwell tonight to meet a man. I'll be back later or tomorrow and move in."

"Jeez," Barney looked confused. "I thought ya needed a place right away."

"I sure do appreciate all you're doin' for me, and I might be back tonight, but I don't know seein' how far it is on to Farwell. I got to see a guy, might have a job for me, but he said to get here today, so I better get."

"Huh," Barney grunted as he turned out the light, locked the door and clumped back down the stairs.

"Maddy," he yelled as he rounded the corner. Maddy opened her door again.

"How about if I pay you for a coupla days," Brant suggested. "I got to go to Farwell, and I might or might not be back tonight, but for sure I'll be back tomorrow," and he worked a twenty dollar bill out of a battered wallet. Maddy had it in her pocket almost before Brant knew it was gone from his fingers.

"Fine with me," she agreed and closed the door on them. Brant heard the bolt slide across. The door was so flimsy, the bolt wouldn't do much good if anyone wanted to break in, but if she felt safer with it, so what.

"Well, okay, Grady. Here's the key. Ya know ya got a place to stay for a coupla days at least, and I'll be seein' ya."

"Sure thing, Barney. Great of you to help out, and I like your friends. See you again." Barney took off, and Brant followed his tail lights out to the highway. The pickup headed south while Brant turned north in the direction of Farwell which was also the direction of Rivermount and home. It had been a useful evening. Tomorrow besides filling Hardin in on Barney, Maddy and the gang at Frank's Bar, he'd come back and carefully sift through the late Jake's room for any clues that might have been left behind.

CHAPTER SEVEN

Next Morning

Early next morning Brant went back to what was now his rented room in Lakeside. Daylight did nothing to improve his impressions from last night. He carried an old Navy duffel bag up the steps. If Maddy was watching, she would think he had brought his gear. Actually all it contained was a pair of work gloves, a flashlight and a few other handy tools.

A dusty pair of windows in the gable end of the room shed somewhat more light than the bulb in the ceiling. Brant had been in grubby living quarters before, but he sighed as he looked around. He found it both disgusting and dispiriting that people lived like this.

A sagging cloth curtain covered an alcove that served as a closet. Brant started his search there with the clothes still hanging in it. Jacob Kowalski's wardrobe had been minimal and thrift shop fashion. A couple of pairs of khaki pants hung on hooks, and three shirts clung to rusty wire hangers.

After checking all the pockets Brant stuffed the clothes in the duffel bag. There was no dresser in the room. An old orange crate stood on end by the head of the bed to serve as a table and a place to put what few other garments there were – an assortment of mismatched socks with T shirts, all dirty. Brant wondered if Jacob had heard of laundromats.

Next to the closet was another alcove under the eaves which served as the bathroom. Brant guessed the word "bathroom" was a misnomer. The moldy pre-fab shower stall was full of cobwebs. Granted, Jacob hadn't been here since last winter, and cobwebs would accumulate. However, since there was no soap in sight and only one small frayed towel, Brant concluded personal cleanliness for Jacob had been no more important than clean clothes. This followed along with the report Hardin had received from the medical examiner.

Brant had found nothing yet that assured him this room had been occupied by the man whose body had been found with the dead elk. So far he was simply proceeding on the assumption that the "Jake" Barney and his friends mentioned was indeed the same person as Jacob Kowalski. Nothing he'd seen or heard contradicted that, but he was hoping he'd find something in the room to make it definite.

Brant turned his attention to the bed. There were no sheets on it, only a lumpy mattress, ratty mattress pad and two moth-eaten blankets. Stuffing spilled out of a hole in the mattress which looked as if some rodent had chewed on it. Brant lifted the mattress off the sagging springs. An envelope lay pressed into a grid by the wires.

It was addressed to Jacob Kowalski, General Delivery, Lakeside. The postmark was from Garberville, California dated in November of last year. Inside was a short letter written in a childish hand.

Dear Daddy,

Our teacher said we should write a letter. How are you? I am fine. Momma says you are working. She said she will put the address on this. She said we are going to move soon. You better come home now or you won't know where we are.

Your son,

Jakey

Sunlight shone through the dusty window as Brant read the letter. A boy somewhere might never know what happened to his father. Maybe Kowalski's family could be traced, but more likely they would have moved on without leaving a forwarding address. Brant sighed again and put the letter in the bag along with the clothes. At least it confirmed that the man who had occupied this room was the one who had been murdered at the elk hunt.

Brant carefully searched the rest of the room. All he found was more dirt. No shoes nor coat besides what had been found on the body. No book, no paper, not even a comic book. He could hear roaches scuttling into cracks ahead of his approach.

He took one last look around, then picked up the duffel bag and went down the steps. He threw the bag in the car, went to the front door and knocked.

Maddy opened it and looked at him blankly.

"Yeah?"

"Mornin'. I'm the guy rented your room last night. Remember me? I came with Barney."

Recognition dawned on Maddy's wrinkled face. "Oh, yeah. Moved in, huh?"

"Well, no. That's what I came to tell you. I won't be needin' the room afterall. I found me a job in Farwell, and a room goes with it so ---."

"I can't give ya no refund since I was holdin' the place for ya for two days," Maddy interrupted him. "Had to turn another guy away on accounta that."

"Oh." Brant said with what he hoped sounded like disappointment. He knew she was lying about the prospect of another roomer, but he'd let her think he believed her. "Well, I guess I'm just outta luck then, but thanks anyway. Maybe I'll see ya sometime again. So long, and here's the key."

Brant backed his car out to the street. As he drove down the road and looked in the rearview mirror, he saw Maddy climbing the outside stairs. She would find her late roomers clothes all gone. It would be interesting to see if she reported the theft.

An hour later he drove into the Justice Center parking lot in Farwell and carried the duffel bag into Hardin's office. Hardin and Chuck guffawed when they saw him.

"Your reputation has preceded you. We just took a complaint from one Maddy Perkins in Lakeside. Seems some guy named Grady Brown just stole all of a roomer's gear from her house. Funny thing, her description of him sounded very much like you. How about that!"

"Good god, it's too much to believe. That old broad actually has the nerve to report it. She's right of course. Here's the stuff." He handed over the duffel bag and sat down to report on his activities.

"You were correct about them being kind of clannish down there. I don't think they would welcome men in uniform much. They're not too particular about hunting out of season either which is probably not news to you."

Brant went on to give Hardin and Chuck a careful report of the previous evening including his dealings with Maddy. "So I'm out twenty bucks to the old bat, but I brought you all Jacob Kowalski's personal effects, including a letter to him from his son who was in Garberville last fall but expecting to move soon. Want to go through the bag?"

Hardin dumped the duffel bag out on the floor. It was a pathetic little pile – all that remained of the life of

Jacob Kowalski. Hardin picked up the letter and looked it over.

"I'll follow up on this. Check the post office in Lakeside. See if they just might be holding any other mail for him. We'll try to get word to the family if the California police can find them. It's barely possible he might have written something to his wife about who he was working with. Obviously he had at least let them know where he was. And Chuck or I'll go have a chat with Maddy about the theft she reported," and Hardin chuckled.

"Don't blow my cover," Brant cautioned. "We might have use for it again sometime. I have an idea nothing much going on in the woods gets past those guys."

"I'll be careful. Your acting skills are much appreciated, and I think we'll need them some more."

CHAPTER EIGHT

Party Invitations

The sun shone from a clear blue sky on a perfect day in May. Brant waved to the Westons who were just leaving the Rivermount post office parking lot as he drove in. Lisl stood by her car as she looked over her mail.

"Good morning," Brant greeted her. "Anything interesting?"

"Hi," she answered. Her smile indicated she was glad to see him.

"Yes." She held up a square envelope. "Go see if you have one of these. Westons had one. It's an invitation to a party."

Brant went on inside the post office and was soon back waving an identical envelope.

"Sounds like a really big bash," he said as he read. "So Sylvia wants to celebrate their tenth anniversary. I suppose it is something of an accomplishment. I have a feeling not everyone thought it would last that long."

"Oh, I don't know," Lisl said. "I think Sylvia and Gerald are perfect for each other. Or should I say, they deserve each other. Anyway, it ought to be lots of fun."

"Since we're both invited, may I have the honor of escorting you, milady?" Brant asked.

"Kind sir, I'd be delighted," Lisl laughed. "I'm sure all our friends will have been invited. Let's plan to go together. It's the week before Memorial Day. I have a couple of conventions coming, but the planning is all done."

Brant whistled softly when Lisl opened her door the night of Sylvia and Gerald Peck's anniversary party.

"You look gorgeous." She wore something silky that clung to her neat figure in just the right places. It was a soft green that complemented her dark hair.

"Thank you," Lisl said, her smile curling up the corners of her mouth. "You look very handsome too." Brant had on dark slacks and a light blue blazer that gave his gray eyes a blue tint. "That coat is just right for you. I knew it would be fun to dress up. We'll hardly recognize all our friends."

The Pecks had rented the Plaza Room at Rivermount Lodge for their party. Floor length windows opened onto an ample deck overlooking one of the lakes on the Lower golf course. The day had been unseasonally hot for May at Rivermount's four thousand feet altitude, and the late sunlight still warmed the air. The smell of pine mingled with mown grass as guests gathered, drinks in hand, to admire the view and each other.

"Darlings, I'm so glad you could come," Sylvia greeted Lisl and Brant. "You both look absolutely too marvelous."

"It's so nice of you to invite us," Lisl murmured, "and your dress is beautiful." It was a lace and silk confection in a peach shade which made Sylvia's blonde hair look almost natural. Lisl immediately assessed the cost of it at something around a thousand dollars. This was the second or third marriage for Sylvia and Gerald – Lisl wasn't sure just how often each of them had previously been married before they tried matrimony together. She saw Gerald's distinguished white hair across the room.

"And, darlings, I have a favor to ask you," Sylvia went on in her breathless, little-girl voice. "I've invited a perfectly lovely man we've known for years. From San

Francisco, you know. He lives there lots of the time, but he has a stunning house and ranch outside Farwell. It's on the river with a spectacular view of the mountains. When I found out he was going to be here now, of course I wanted him to share our celebration. I've put him at the table with you and your friends. I know you'll like him and take good care of him. His name is Colman Lewis, or is it Lewis Colman?" Sylvia looked vague. "Oh well, you'll find out, won't you, dears?" and she turned to greet more guests.

Lisl and Brant procured drinks from the bartender and headed for the deck. Westons were already there with the Michaels. After they'd admired each other's attire and commented on how great they looked, they settled down to do the same with the other guests. Rivermount was a small enough community that they knew nearly everyone living there.

"I understand that Sylvia has entrusted a single man to our care," Lisl remarked. "She said they know him from when they lived in San Francisco. Said he's a dear friend except that she couldn't remember his name for sure. Colman Lewis or Lewis Colman. I'm not sure Sylvia always has her head on straight."

"Oh, I've already met him," Angie Michaels told her. "It's Colman for the first name. He seems very nice. He's over there talking to the Shedds, the tall, bald man in the white dinner jacket."

"Jeez, what a party!" Phil Campbell said as he and Elaine joined their friends. "I hate to think what it will do to Gerald's bank balance. Beaucoup bucks! But great food," as he helped himself to a tidbit from a tray of elegant canapes being passed by a waiter.

"And what a perfect night," Caro said. "It's not often we get such a warm evening in May. Look at the mountains still so white with snow while we're acting like it's mid-summer."

The head waiter circulated among the crowd gently suggesting they find their tables since dinner was to be served.

"I know where we are," Angie said. "I looked around when we came in. It's over there," and she led her friends to a spot near the windows where they could watch the sun setting beyond the mountains. Lisl found her place card between Brant and Sylvia's friend. He joined them as they were sorting out who sat where.

Introductions were accomplished, and Brant reached to hold Lisl's chair for her only to find Colman had beat him to it and was already deep in conversation with her. Brant felt a little scowl crease his forehead. The man was impressive looking with piercing blue eyes which contrasted with his tanned bald head. Brant decided Colman must have been a blond before his hair went south.

"Lisl. That's a lovely name. Just right for you," Colman was saying. Lisl smiled her thank you. "And what keeps your days busy in this delightful place? Golf and bridge?"

Lisl laughed gently. "No, not exactly. I'm the convention manager for the resort. It leaves me enough time for a golf game now and then, hikes, skiing in the winter, bridge not very often."

"How fortunate you are to find work you like in such an attractive environment." He turned to Caro sitting on his left. "And you, do you also work here?"

"Only volunteer jobs. The rest of us are retired. Lisl is the only one not old enough for that yet. Jud and I retired a couple of years ago. Jud was a mechanical engineer, and I taught kindergarten. Doc was in family medicine in Portland, and Angie was a nurse. Phil was with the U.S. Fish and Wildlife, and Elaine taught junior high. Brant was a detective with a police department over in the valley. Now you know all about us, what about you?"

Colman smiled. "Thank you for your quick biographies. I'm sure I don't know all the interesting things there are to know about you, but I'll hope to get better acquainted. As for me, I'm in the export-import business."

"That sounds interesting," Lisl said. "Just what do you export and import?"

"Oh, very mundane things, lumber, foods, machinery, things like that going out, and clothes, textiles, toys, art objects, etc. coming back."

"And Sylvia said you live most of the time in San Francisco?"

"That's where my mail comes, but I'm rarely there. I'm out of the country a good share of the time, and when I can grab some free time, I'm up here at my ranch."

"I suppose you have someone who runs the ranch for you?" Lisl asked.

"Yes, an excellent crew. There's the manager, ranch foreman, and a Mexican couple who take care of the house. Other workmen are hired as needed. We raise alfalfa and hay, but mainly horses. And some llamas just for fun. Do you like to ride?"

"It's been a long time since I've had much opportunity, but I love to."

First time I ever knew that, Brant thought to himself as Colman went on talking.

"Then you'll have to come out to the ranch and join me someday. In fact, I'd be pleased to have all of you come for dinner. I know so few people in this area. I'd like to get better acquainted. Do you like game? I have some choice elk in the freezer from last hunting season."

"I've never had elk," Caro said. "I'd like to try it." The others agreed with her.

"Fine," Colman said, "Then it's settled. I have to go to Hong Kong tomorrow. How about the Sunday of Memorial Day weekend?"

"Sounds good to me," Phil said. "Okay with everybody?"

"I'm so glad," Colman said with a warm smile which lingered on Lisl. "I'll have my manager send you a note with instructions for finding the house. Shall we say seven o'clock? Then it will still be light enough for you to enjoy the view. And now," he turned to Lisl, "tell me about the convention business here. Is it busy this year?"

Brant knew he was scowling, and he didn't care. This character was monopolizing Lisl's attention. She'd hardly said boo to him since they sat down. Oh well, the food was good. He could talk to Lisl later.

"Oh look," Angie said. "They have a band. How neat. I love to dance."

The food had been delicious, the wine plentiful, and the guests were feeling content. Time for a couple of anniversary toasts while the band set up their instruments.

George Shedd stepped to the microphone and said all the usual kind words about Sylvia and Gerald along with a few jokes. The hosts replied gracefully, the band tuned up, and Gerald led Sylvia to the dance floor inviting everyone to join them. Brant turned to Lisl only to find himself a moment late again. She was moving out to the floor with Colman.

"Hey, you're going to have to watch that," Phil said to Brant. "If you don't move fast that smooth guy will steal your girl."

Brant laughed, but he wasn't sure it sounded like a laugh. More like he was gargling. Or growling. He could hear Angie and Elaine across the table commenting on what a striking couple Lisl and Colman made and such good dancers.

The music stopped, and Lisl and Colman returned to the table. Brant decided to be prompt this time.

"How about the next dance with me?" he asked.

"I'd love to," Lisl agreed, and her smile made the evening right again.

Colman dutifully danced with the other ladies at the table, then took himself off the dance with his hostess. Brant had to acknowledge to himself that the man had good manners. And it would be interesting to see his ranch.

"This Cinderella's coach is going to turn into a pumpkin if we don't go home soon," Angie said. "It's been a large evening. I think I've danced my feet off up to the ankles. We don't stay up this late very often."

"I think you're right," Lisl said, "and I have to go to work for awhile tomorrow even though it's Sunday." She turned to Brant. "Should we go say our "thank yous" and "best wishes" to the Peck's?"

Brant held her chair as she stood up. "It's been so very nice to meet you," she said to Colman. "Thank you for your lovely invitation to dinner. I know we'll all look forward to it. Have a good time in Hong Kong, and we'll see you when you come back."

Colman took her hand and held it longer than Brant thought was necessary, but he could afford to be generous now since it was he, not Colman, seeing Lisl home.

"Oh, it's going to be good to get these shoes off," Lisl said as Brant turned into her driveway. "Come in a few minutes, and we can wind down from the party. I'm too wound up to go to sleep right away. I haven't danced so much since I was in college."

Why not accept her invitation, Brant thought, why not, indeed. He opened her car door and then the house door.

"Would you like a taste of brandy?" Lisl asked.

"I need more to drink like a dog needs fleas, but it sounds good anyway."

Lisl poured two small glasses from a decanter on her buffet and brought them into the living room. She sank onto the sofa, kicked off her shoes, wiggled her toes luxuriously and sipped the brandy.

"Here, come sit by me," she told Brant as he headed for the big chair. "You're too far away over there. What did you think of the evening?"

"Like Phil said, it will put a dent in Peck's bank account, but it was a smashing party. Haven't been to one that fancy in years."

"I couldn't stand doing that every night, but it's really terrific once in awhile. And what did you think of Colman?"

The little scowl came back between Brant's eyes. "I don't know. He's okay, I guess. Seems nice enough. It should be interesting to see his place."

"He certainly leads a cosmopolitan existence flying off to Hong Kong so casually. I'll bet he has some interesting souvenirs."

"Sounds like he's a hunter too if we're having elk for dinner. But changing the subject," Brant wasn't very interested in talking about Colman Lewis, "do you want to play golf tomorrow? I have a tee time right after noon. I think Westons want to play."

"That'd be great." She stretched and yawned. "This is so relaxing after our active evening." Her head rested on Brant's shoulder. His arm slipped around her, and his lips brushed her hair.

"You look so beautiful tonight. I hate to call an end to the party."

"You don't have to, you know." She snuggled closer to him. "You could stay here."

"That possibility had crossed my mind. Are you sure you want to go that route?" He moved enough to look at Lisl's face, to try to see what he could read there. "I'm not much for the one-night stand routine."

"No, I didn't think you were, and neither am I, but yes, I think I'm sure."

"Lisl," Brant looked at her carefully, "we've known each other since last winter, but we don't know a lot about each other before that. I know you came from Kansas, you went to college there and were married, the marriage didn't work out, you went into hotel work and were transferred here. You know that I've lived in Oregon all my life, was in the Navy, went to college here, became a policeman, was married and widowed, have two children and am retired now. Do we need to know more?"

Lisl shook her head tentatively. "Do we?" she asked.

"Well, for instance," Brant went on, "how do you feel about marriage since you tried it once and it didn't work? I'm finding you an increasing presence in my life, and I don't want to take a wrong step."

"Brant, you are such a dear person, and I've come to like you very, very much. I know that your wife left you a legacy of a wonderful life together. You haven't talked about her with me, but I can tell she was a treasure just from your casual conversation." Brant nodded.

"And my marriage – it was a case of being in love with love, I think. Somehow the attraction didn't survive real life. It seems so long ago. I think marriage can be wonderful, but I don't want to take that step quite yet. Let's let the past be past and start from here. I feel like we're ready for our acquaintance to move to something more. Can you feel that?"

She moved out of the circle of his arm and turned to him. Her hands held his face gently as she looked questioningly into his eyes. Then her hands slid down to his chest. Brant felt a wave of emotion wash over him like he hadn't felt in many months.

"Of course you're right," he said. "I'm an old worrier, too concerned about things that aren't relevant. It's time to move on."

Lisl stood up, held out her hand to Brant, and he followed her into the bedroom.

CHAPTER NINE

Late May

"Brant, Hardin here."

"Hi, what can I do for you?"

"I'm thinking it's about time for Grady Brown to visit his friends in Lakeside again. How about coming in to the office in the near future, and we'll set it up?"

Brant sat down across the desk from Hardin and Chuck. "What exactly do you have in mind?"

"We've come to a stop on this elk hunt investigation. Bunch of dead ends. If Grady makes another visit down south, maybe we can stir up some action."

"What about the robbery I did?"

Chuck laughed. "I was delegated to follow up on that. After Maddy finished giving me her tale of woe about your having stolen her roomer's worldly goods, I told her it sounded like you did her a favor removing the garbage. She was kinda huffy, but I calmed her down when I said we'd keep looking for you and would try to return the stuff to his wife, and Maddy was a good citizen to report the theft of someone else's property. When she realized she wasn't going to get anything out of it in any event, she lost interest. She didn't know any more about the guy than we already knew."

"How about the widow? Were you able to find her?"

"Yeah, but it didn't do any good. The Garberville cops were about as helpful as I could have expected. She's moved out of town but was still working as a waitress in town so it didn't take long for them to find her. He'd never been much use as a husband or father, so I guess she didn't care too deeply that he wasn't coming back. He'd written her just once saying he was going to come into some big money, but she'd heard that story before and wasn't expecting anything. There wasn't any mention of where or how he planned to get this money or who he was working with except that he met the person at a bar. Nothing new there. That only agrees with what we already knew. So I think it's time to stir the pot and see what comes of it."

"And what's my story about where I've been and what I've been doing?"

"Now it just so happens I've not been idle," Hardin answered. "I have your job and your living quarters all arranged."

"Uh huh, tell me about it."

"You managed to get a job with a highway paving crew. Hot, messy, dirty work, but it keeps you eating. You've rented a room from a nice, little old lady in the low rent end of town. So you have some money in your pocket, and you just decided to come down and see how the guys are doing, and just incidentally see how the prospects are for hunting maybe out of season. When the antlers are still in velvet, you can get big money selling them in the Orient for an aphrodisiac."

"Okay, but what if someone should want to check up on my story? I think lying comes so naturally to that gang that they'll assume everyone else does it too."

"Oh, I've fixed that too. You're working for Morgan Paving, and I know the owner there. He knows about you and will tell anyone who asks that you're not working that day and he doesn't know where you are. Your landlady is a dear, name's Elsie Swenson, and she'll give anyone asking about you a run-around like you've got a girl friend and stay at her house sometimes or whatever. She even has some clothes to hang in a closet that look like what Grady Brown would wear. And they'll both let us know if someone comes asking for you. Have I missed anything?"

"No, I guess you've covered all my objections. When do you want this to come off?"

"How about tomorrow night – Friday night? Those bums are sure to be in Frank's place on a Friday. That is," Hardin thought belatedly, "unless you have some other plans."

Brant cracked a one-sided smile. "Nice of you to ask, but no, I'm free. My girl has a big convention going down this weekend and is tied up until Sunday night."

"Lisl's your girl now, huh. I knew your social life was improving, but I didn't know it had come to that," and Hardin grinned.

"Looks better every day," Brant assured him,. "except for that rancher we met the other night. I think he'd like to beat me out. You ever heard of Colman Lewis?"

"Colman Lewis? Sounds familiar. Oh, yeah, I know who you mean – you know, Chuck? That guy who bought the old Western Bar S ranch a few years ago. Where'd you meet him?"

"At a big dinner party last week. He's invited all of us – Westons, Michaels, Campbells and Lisl and me to an elk dinner Sunday night. What do you know about him?"

"Not much really. He's here only occasionally, I guess. Has a fair size staff who run the place but very low key. Doesn't attract attention. There's an electric gate on the road, and we've never had any reason to get in so I haven't seen the place since he bought it. You can't see it from the road at all. He rebuilt the old ranch house almost totally, I've heard. Raises horses and a few llamas and a little feed. He bought the whole ranch, more'n a thousand acres, but I guess he's using only a small part of it. So he took a shine to Lisl, huh?"

"He's invited her to come horseback riding sometime. It'll be interesting to see the place from what you say. Where is it?"

"Take the road out of town west and at the junction turn left around the base of the hill. You'll come to the gate part way up the grade. I'd like to know what you think of the operation."

"I'll give you a report. And tomorrow night Grady Brown is up for a big night in Lakeside. See you later."

CHAPTER TEN

Friday of Memorial Day Weekend

The gravel parking lot at Frank's Bar was full. Noise and smoke drifted out the open door to hang in the night air around the blinking red neon sign. Hardin had been right. Friday night was busy. Brant parked at the end of the lot almost in the bushes. He recognized Barney's pick-up as he headed for the door.

"Well, look who's here," a raucous voice yelled. Brant squinted in the nicotine haze and found Barney holding up the far end of the bar. "Thought you'd forgot your Lakeside friends."

The words were slightly slurred - sounded as if Barney had been here awhile. Brant ambled his way over and shook hands.

"Howya doin', Barney?"

"Where ya been all this time? Found a job?"

"Yep, got me a job with a pavin' outfit. Crummy but it's a job. With the guy I told ya about. Figured I'd come down and see how all you guys are doin'," and he surveyed the room. At the usual table in the corner he recognized the men he'd met before. Couldn't remember all their names, but it didn't matter. They were all old friends now.

"Lemme buy ya another beer. Two Buds," he told Frank. "Gotta say hello to all the guys." When the beers came, the two men moved through the crowd to join the corner group.

Everyone he remembered seemed to be there. It was a little hard to tell in the dim light.

"What's up with you guys?" he asked.

"Joe here's been drivin' a log truck. Lucky guy. Not too many of those jobs open 'lessen you know someone," Barney said. "I got my alfalfa planted. Gonna be a good year. After all the winter snow we got plentya water for a change. Now I'm thinkin' about fishin' or maybe," he lowered his voice, "maybe a little target shootin', know what I mean," and he nudged Brant.

"Uh, yeah, I guess I get ya. But in summer?"

Barney sniggered. "Fall time ya get the big racks to sell, but in the summer ya get the velvet on them antlers, and them Chinks over in China think that makes 'em great in the sack." Barney sniggered again and leered at Brant. "Don't make as much as sellin' a big mounted head, but it ain't peanuts neither. Ya wanna go out?"

"Well, yeah, I guess so. If I can get off work." Brant studied his hands. He'd been careful to rub dirt and grease on them appropriate for someone working on the highways.

"Where ya say you're working?"

"Morgan Paving. Don't work every day. When ya thinkin' about?"

"When ya get a day off in the middle a the week, gimme a call. Or I'll call you when it looks good. I'll hafta scout around to find the herds. Who ya workin' for? How can I get ya? Where ya livin'?"

"Clem Morgan's the boss. He'll know where I am. I'm livin' on Jepston Street, 340. Nice room. Better'n what ya showed me with Maddy."

Barney guffawed. "Didn't like Maddy's place, huh? You're right, it ain't great."

"I'm not too fussy, but when I got the dough, I don't wanna share with the cockroaches. And that old broad is so godawful ugly she'd scare a Halloween spook.

Landlady I got now is a nice old dear. She don't bother me none, and I don't give her any trouble."

Brant drank some more of his beer and glanced around the table.

"Ya need a refill?" Barney had emptied his bottle again and so had some of the others. "Hey, Frank, some a the folks over here are dry."

Frank brought the fresh bottles, and Brant tossed a couple of twenties on the table.

"Well, that's mighty nice a ya, Grady," Kenny said.

Grady Brown felt magnanimous. He turned the subject back to hunting. "How are the cops or game wardens or whatever ya got around here?"

"Better'n they oughta be," the old man said. "They don't wanna take a little on the side. When I was a kid, ya'd give 'em a few bucks and they'd look th'other way."

"Yeah, and they're getting' crafty," Kenny went on. "Even set up decoys. Now that's downright dishonest."

"No! How's that work?" Brant asked.

"You ain't done much huntin' if ya haven't seen that," Kenny went on. "Why last fall right in the middle of huntin' season, I had me a deer tag all legal like. Come down the road and seen this buck and doe right out in the open. Me an' my partner fired three shots outta the truck and damned if the fuckin' cops weren't right on us. Course it ain't legal to fire outta the truck, but hell, if ya take time to get out, the damn deer woulda been off and runnin'. Except as it turned out that buck and doe weren't even alive. Just stuffed. The cops are death on road hunters if they can catch 'em, but I think puttin' out decoys ain't fair. Cost me 250 bucks which I didn't have so I tried to fight it, but turned out they had a camera hid in the bushes. Goddam fuckin' thieves, they are, takin' money from us poor folks."

Brant nodded attentively and looked sympathetic to Kenny's tale of the devious law enforcement authorities meanwhile thinking to himself, if you weren't too lazy to get out of your truck, you wouldn't have had the problem.

Tales of hunting prowess went around the table. Most of them involved various degrees of illegal activities along with outrage at the cops for their efforts in thwarting the whole process. Brant injected "no kiddin'" and clucks of amazement at suitable places while his mind moved between anger and amusement.

Barney nudged him again. "Need another beer?"

Brant had learned through the years to seem to be drinking while actually making one beer last a long time. One bottle wouldn't last forever, though, and by now he'd finished the first one.

"Yeah, guess I could use another," and he started to signal Frank.

"No, lemme get thish one," Barney slurred. "You been buyin' 'em all. Come on over t'the bar. Wanna talk to ya."

Brant and Barney moved with their empty bottles from the table to a place by themselves at the end of the bar. A doorway behind them led out to the storeroom. Frank brought refills, and Barney looked around to be sure no one was listening. His gestures were so obvious that Brant had all he could do to keep from laughing. Barney was telling the world that he was about to say something secret. No one seemed to care except possibly Frank who glanced their way quickly.

"I gotta proposhishun for ya." Barney leaned over close, and Brant smelled the stale odor of many beers. "Now I got my alfalfa in, lesh set up a deer or elk hunt. Make a little extra. Whaddya say?"

"Sounds good, but I don't have any equipment 'cept a rifle. Where we goin'?"

"Just leave it all to me. Th'guy I work with – he's got everythin'. Horses, truck, whatever. Got him a big dual wheel. Proud as punch with that truck."

"How you gonna get it set up then?"

"Ya just leave that to me. I'll send 'im a letter."

"A letter? Where in hell is he?"

"This dude is real careful. He don't want no one to know where he lives. He's the one sells the stuff, an' he ain't eager to spend time in the slammer. He's got all the gear. We jus' go along an' shoot. Make some money, an' we don't shee 'im again until the next time."

"What's his name?"

"You don't even need to know that. I call 'im Jer, but I shend the letters to Jack Jones at a box in Farwell, an' he picks 'em up and then he calls me an' we get somethin' goin'. It'll take awhile to get it all set up which is okay since it's too early in the season for the antlers yet. July'll be about right. I'll write 'im an' tell 'im I found a guy wants to help out. Then I'll call you. Ya got a phone?"

"No, but ya can leave a message with Elsie – my landlady, ya know. Sounds kinda complicated, though," and Brant shook his head dubiously.

"Hey, no problem. It'll work out jus' fine, you'll see. Always has ever' time before. So whaddya say your address is? Hey, Frank, gimme a piece a paper an' somethin' to write with."

Frank produced a scrap of paper and a stubby pencil from behind the cash register, and Barney laboriously wrote Grady Brown's address and phone number down as Brant spelled it out for him.

There now, thash all set," and Barney whacked Brant's shoulder. "Les' go talk to th'guys shomemore," and he stumbled back to the table in the corner.

CHAPTER ELEVEN

Saturday

Brant had his hand on the doorknob when the phone rang. For a moment he considered not answering it. What is it about a ringing phone that's almost impossible to ignore, he reflected as he picked up the receiver.

"Glad I found you home," Hardin said.

"You almost didn't. I was just going out the door to go hit a bucket of balls at the driving range. My golf game needs some work."

"Forget it. Your golf game is just fine from what I've seen, and I need you. I'll pick you up in about fifteen minutes."

"Hey, whoa, what's this all about?"

"Some fisherman reported another body up by the lakes. Shot in the back of the head. Sound familiar?"

"Uh-oh. Why don't I meet you at the grocery store parking lot and save you the time coming to my house?"

"Good idea. See you."

Brant stepped out of his car as he saw the sheriff's department pick-up turn into the parking lot.

"Fill me in on this," Brant said as he slid in beside Hardin.

"Like I said, a fisherman taking a short cut between lakes on an old logging road saw the body in the ditch. He called from somewhere, and we sent our closest deputy out to talk to him and wait until we get there. All I know so far is that the body sure didn't die of natural causes."

"You think it might be connected to our elk affair?"

"Who knows yet, but it sounds like it might. Incidentally, Barney Valent was out early this morning checking up on you. He was at Morgan Paving asking for Grady Brown, and he went to see Elsie too. Left a message with her for you."

"What did my employer and landlady tell him?"

"Your boss told him you weren't working today, and he didn't know where you were. Elsie told him somewhat the same – said you hadn't come home last night, and she sort of thought you might have a girl friend somewhere. She said she'd see you got the message. I hope it all satisfied him that you're for real. Tell me about your night out at Frank's. I got your message this morning," Hardin said.

"I found out Barney and his buddies don't much like lawmen. They think we're downright dishonest when we put out decoys to catch the road hunters. Barney was drunk enough to not be as careful as he might have been about trying to pull me into a deer or elk hunt for antlers in velvet. The person who runs the show is called Jer and is very secretive. Barney gets in touch with him via mail at a P.O. box in Farwell under the name of Jack Jones. Then Jer calls to make the arrangements. He provides what's needed, truck, horses, whatever, and he's the one who sells the stuff giving Barney and whoever else a cut. Not much to go on. Barney was planning to scout out where the herds might be. I was just supposed to wait until I heard from him again. What was the message he left with Elsie?"

"To come down to the tavern again Tuesday night."

"Okay. We'll see what cooks."

The pick-up jounced onto a gravel road and then to a rutted dirt one.

"I'm glad you know where you're going out here. I had no idea there were so many little roads that aren't on anyone's map," Brant said.

Hardin turned another corner. "Here we are." A sheriff's car sat by the side of the road with a young deputy leaning against it.

Hardin introduced Brant. "So what do we have, Gary?"

"Body's right here," the officer said as he walked around his car. "I talked to the man who found him, got his name and address and all that. He was pretty upset, in a big hurry to get away from it all. When I asked him if he touched anything, he said 'no way'. He didn't seem to know anything about it except that he just happened to see it."

Brant and Hardin looked at the body lying face down in the shallow ditch with a bullet hole in the back of his head. Brant whistled.

"It's Barney."

"You're sure? Not much face left," Hardin said as he turned the man over.

"Even without the face, yes, I'm sure. Same clothes, build, there couldn't be another just like him. Any identification on him?" he asked Gary.

"I haven't looked. I didn't want to touch anything until you got here."

Hardin felt in Barney's pockets and pulled out a billfold. "Yeah, it's him. Here's his driver's license. Now what does all this tell us?"

He squatted on his heels and rubbed his hand over his face.

"How long ago are you thinking?" Brant asked.

"Not long, no sign of rigor. In fact, he's still slightly warm. I think maybe we're in luck again. This road is seldom used. He might easily have been here for days before someone happened along."

"For sure he was alive last night even if pretty much pickled in alcohol, and this morning too, checking up on Grady. First Jacob Kowalski and now Barney. Someone sure takes the direct route to get rid of people. When I first heard of Jacob at the tavern, something was said about him talking and bragging around there before he turned up missing. It'd be my guess somebody thought Barney was talking too much last night. I wonder who put the finger on him. Could it be possible the mysterious 'Jer' is actually one of the men in that group?"

"That'd be nice to know. Think about it and maybe it'll come to you. Let's look around here. From the hole in his head, Barney was standing up when he was shot, but I don't think he was standing here in the ditch. He's been rolled over. Tire tracks have messed it up some, but I'd guess he was about here in the middle of the road."

"Interesting that there isn't a cartridge casing," Brant commented. "Whoever did it is being more careful this time. No bullet to match with the others. It was from short range, certainly."

"Well, fan out and let's see if we find anything else."

Brant walked back along the edge of the road. In the damp earth of the ditch he found tire prints of a dual wheel truck.

"Hardin," he called, "here's something – tire tracks. Can you get somebody out here to make casts of these? I think they'll turn out to match what we found before. And I'll give you even money that Barney's boots match one set we had. What I called the logger's boots. That leaves the cowboy boots still unaccounted for."

"There's no way to tell which direction he might have been facing when he got shot. Trying to find the spent cartridge would be like looking for a needle in a haystack," Hardin said as he surveyed the surrounding brush and trees.

"Probably was facing right on up the road," Brant guessed. "Whoever did it rolled him over off the road, but it isn't likely he would have turned him end for end. Maybe we can spot splintered wood on a tree."

"Hey, Lieutenant," Gary called from just off the road in the woods. "Here it is, the bullet."

Hardin hurried over. "Well, would you look at that. What'd I just say about needles in haystacks? Look, Brant, Gary's found it. Flattened and mashed in this tree, but we'll get it cut out. Great work, Gary. We'll make a detective out of you yet."

"Next move is to get a search warrant for Valent's house and notify the widow, I guess," Brant said.

"Yeah. Gary, you stay here until the men come out to make the casts of those tire prints and get the bullet. We'll take Barney back to town with us and get him on his way to the medical examiner in Portland. Come on, Brant. I have a feeling it's going to be a long day."

As they neared Rivermount, Brant said, "Just drop me off, and I'll go on home."

"Hell, no," Hardin answered. "I want you along when we go to Valent's. You have a good eye for what might be interesting."

"But that'll blow my Grady Brown cover."

"Oh, jeez, you're right. I forgot about Grady for a minute. And I guess we do still want Grady to exist. Someone might put two and two together if he just disappeared right now. They might think Grady was the one who shot Barney and then beat it. Oh well, I'll get someone else."

"I wonder if you'll find Barney's rifle at his house or in his truck. It'd be nice to be able to check the ballistics on it. Do you want me to keep that date with Barney for next Tuesday night?"

"Sure do."

CHAPTER TWELVE

Sunday Dinner

Sunday evening Brant picked up Lisl and then the Campbells for their dinner party with Colman Lewis.

"Do you know where we're going?" Elaine asked.

"Yes," Lisl answered. "Colman's ranch manager sent me a note with instructions. We're going to meet Westons and Michaels at the junction west of town, and they can follow us."

"Sounds good," Phil said. "I really want to see this place. I've heard a lot about it. Say, Brant, did you see the item in the paper this morning about someone finding another body yesterday? Up in the lake area somewhere. Hardin was quoted, said the man had been shot in the back of the head. Name was Barney something."

"No, I didn't happen to see it," Brant answered, which was true enough. He hadn't read the local paper thoroughly. In any event, he didn't want to discuss another murder tonight. Time enough later to do that. He hadn't heard yet from Hardin what they might have found when they went to Valent's house.

Westons and Michaels were waiting at the junction when Brant came by. Everyone waved, and Jud pulled in behind Brant to follow him up the hill. Around the turn and out of sight of the highway they came to the gate marking the ranch entrance. A speaker box was mounted on a post in front of the gate. Brant told the voice from the box who they were, and the heavy metal gate slid smoothly aside.

They crossed a bridge over the river, and from there the road curved on up the hill until they rounded one more bend. The ranch buildings spread out in front of them.

Phil whistled softly. "I smell money, lots of it," he said as he looked at the complex.

To the left were stables along with other farm buildings, a small house, and a large hay storage shed. Directly ahead up the drive was the ranch house with garages on the left end.

"It's gorgeous," Lisl breathed. "Fits the terrain perfectly."

Brant parked the car, and Jud pulled in alongside. As they all moved toward the front door, Brant had to admit it was pretty spectacular. The hill continued upward for a short distance toward the north beyond the far end of the house. Half a dozen tall ponderosa pines cast long shadows across the drive in the early evening sun. Landscaping had been artfully done with native shrubs, lava rocks and old juniper stumps to give a natural effect. The garage wing formed a shallow V with the house shutting off the sight of the outbuildings. Built of wood and river rock, the house integrated beautifully with the high desert landscape.

"Look at this front door, would you!" Caro exclaimed. It was of copper embossed in an Indian design. As they approached the entrance, a Mexican man opened the door. Colman came across the slate entry toward them.

"Thank you, Esteban," he said to the Mexican. "Come in, come in all of you. Wonderful to have you here. Isn't it a perfect night? I ordered the weather especially for the occasion."

He ushered them into a spacious foyer with a stairway curving upward on one side. Doors to the left probably went to the garage and other work rooms, Brant guessed. Ahead, louvered doors let a striped pattern of sunlight onto the hall floor and showed the dining table beyond. To the right was the great room where Colman was leading them.

"Fantastic!" Angie said as they took in the view through the wall of windows facing west. The entire jagged spine of central Oregon's Cascade Mountains spread out in a panorama before them.

"Colman, it's just too beautiful for words," Lisl said. "This is a one-in-a-million location."

Colman smiled with pleasure at their delight. "Let's go outside now while it's still warm enough before the sun goes down."

He led the way out onto a stone terrace arranged with comfortable furniture. Grass sloped down to a swimming pool tucked into a curve of the hill. At the edge of the lawn a rail fence marked the nearest pasture where horses and llamas grazed. Beyond that were fields of crops just getting started. The huge spindly wheels of the irrigation system glinted in the sun with the sprinkling water making little rainbows. In the distance forest took over. There was no other house in sight.

Esteban came onto the terrace with a cart containing the makings for drinks. "Do sit down and make yourselves comfortable," Colman said. "Esteban will be happy to fix whatever you like."

When everyone had a drink in hand, a Mexican woman came with a tray of assorted hot and cold canapes. "This is Octavia," Colman introduced her. "She's my treasure of a cook."

"I can see why," Doc said as he tasted one of the tidbits. "This is great."

"Delicious," Angie said. "Does she share recipes?"

"I think you might have some trouble following them," Colman laughed. "She speaks very little English, and I expect her recipes are mostly in Spanish in her head."

For a moment everyone was silent, savoring the good food and drink as well as the perfect scene spread out before them. A few wisps of pink clouds floated over the mountains, now almost in silhouette with the sun sinking behind them.

Lisl broke the quiet. She noticed a curious llama surveying them from the fence line.

"I love the llamas, their sweet faces. They seem much friendlier than their camel cousins. Look at that one. I think he'd like to join the party."

"Would you like to meet him?" Colman invited. He and Lisl walked across the lawn to make the llama's acquaintance.

As they went out of hearing, Phil needled Brant. "You've really got some competition here, fella. This is some spread. That guy has everything, and he may make off with your girl too."

Brant smiled as if he took the remark as a joke, but inside he was thinking Phil was right. How could an ex-policeman compete with all this? The green-eyed monster of jealousy poked into his head.

That first night he'd stayed at Lisl's house had been all he could have hoped for. They'd managed an encore a few nights later, and he was becoming accustomed to the idea. Now an uneasy thought stabbed into his mind that Colman might steal Lisl away from him.

Esteban attentively topped up their drinks and then brought out a platter with a large piece of meat. He lighted a barbecue and went back to the kitchen.

"Gee, look at that hunk of meat," Jud said. "Is that elk?"

"I suppose so since that's what we're invited for," Brant answered as he got up to look at the meat more closely. As he neared the table, he stumbled a bit and put out his hand to steady himself.

"Oops, stuck my hand in the plate. Sorry," as he pulled out his handkerchief to wipe off the meat juice.

Esteban returned with a tray of marinade and seasonings which he spread over the meat coating it on all sides. Lisl and Colman came back to rejoin the group. The shadows lengthened and then disappeared as the sun went behind the mountains. A chill of night crept up with the fading light.

"Let's go inside," Colman suggested, "before it gets too cold. Esteban will go ahead with the cooking while we finish our drinks."

When the guests had arrived, they'd been so mesmerized by the outdoor view that they hadn't really seen the great room. Now it was time to exclaim about it. A large stone fireplace was centered on the wall opposite the windows with comfortable sofas and chairs surrounding a round table of heavy glass supported by elk antlers.

Most of the furniture was ranch house style, wood and homespun fabric. Here and there were pieces of foreign origin. At the north end of the room were two large windows with a black lacquer table between them. An exquisite jade figurine of a Japanese woman in flowing kimono and parasol rested on the table.

At the opposite end of the room stood a folding screen intricately carved of wood illustrating a Chinese fable. An antique chest inlaid with ivory sat along one wall. In another corner a contemporary ivory and ebony chess set sat ready for a game on a table of inlaid exotic woods. Over the mantel an embroidered silk wall hanging depicted golden koi swimming gracefully in a pond.

Brant noted all the beautiful objects, but a mounted elk head on the wall beside the fireplace held his attention. It was huge. Phil spoke quietly behind him. "That is one magnificent specimen, huh? I've never seen a better one in all my years in the woods."

As Brant studied the elk head, he could hear Colman telling the others about the various items – what he called his souvenirs. They had made a circuit of the room and were now seeing the elk.

"What an immense elk head," Caro exclaimed. "Did you shoot it yourself?" she asked her host.

"Oh, yes," he assured her, "just last fall."

"But what a shame to kill such a beautiful creature," Caro mourned. "I don't think I could ever do it."

"Ah, but they can't all live forever, you know," Colman told her. "This one had a long life for an elk, and it was time for him to make room for younger blood."

"That's got to be at least a 340 point Boone and Crockett," Phil guessed.

"Three fifty," Colman corrected him.

"What in heaven's name do Boone and Crockett have to do with this?" Angie wanted to know. "Are we talking about Daniel Boone and Davy Crockett?"

"Yes, actually we are," Colman answered. "There is a club of sportsmen named after Daniel Boone and Davy Crockett. They've set up a rating system for North American trophy heads of all kinds – deer, elk, moose, bear, big horn sheep, pronghorn antelope, whatever else you can think of. Different species have different standards, of course. For elk, points are given for size, spread of antlers, thickness, deduct for uneven, that sort of thing. There's a form to fill out. Anything over about 340 for elk is very good."

"Well, it certainly is a beautiful specimen even if I wouldn't want I myself," Caro conceded.

Octavia came into the room with a tray of thin slices of wheat bread topped with Scottish smoked salmon.

"When I was in England awhile back," Colman told them, "my hostess for dinner one night said she had heard it was considered very smart to serve the first course in the lounge. So I decided we'd have our fish course here while the elk is cooking."

"This is different from our Northwest smoked salmon," Angie said.

"Yes, it's not as heavily smoked and is always sliced very thin rather than in chunks. I like both kinds," Colman replied.

"And is it really from Scotland?" Caro wanted to know.

"Oh, yes, I brought it with me from San Francisco, imported directly."

Was there anything this guy didn't have or do perfectly? Brant wondered. The house, the furnishings, the food, the whole place. The smell of meat cooking on the barbecue drifted in through the open doors. He was trying to pace himself with all the hors d'oeuvres and now the salmon, not wanting to get so full he couldn't eat his dinner.

"You travel so much," Lisl commented. "Do you ever get tired of it – living out of a suitcase?"

"Yes and no," Colman answered. "It's mostly on business, and I have long since quit sightseeing in the usual sense. I enjoy the business challenges, but I'm always happy to come here to feel at home."

Esteban announced dinner, and Colman escorted Lisl to the dining room leaving the others to follow along. The table was a long oval of polished wood set so that all the diners could enjoy the last of the mountain view fading in a pink haze. Lisl was seated on her host's right while Brant found himself at the far end of the table. He made a determined effort not to be angry. Just relax and enjoy the evening, and keep your eyes open, he told himself.

The table was set with hand-woven place mats in a plaid of soft pastels. Fresh spring tulips and iris echoed the colors. The crystal, china and silverware were elegant without being ostentatious. On the end wall opposite the windows hung another silk scroll similar to the one over the fireplace in the great room. This one showed birds and flowers. An antique Oriental buffet stood along one wall. Nothing else adorned the room, nothing to distract from the view outside.

A salad of assorted greens topped by a nasturtium blossom rested at each place with a tart chardonnay already poured in the wine glasses.

"Wherever did you get nasturtiums this time of year?" Angie asked. "They don't grow very well here."

"We have a small green house out in back, and Esteban is an expert horticulturalist."

"And all the different and unusual salad greens – is that where they come from too?"

"Yes, he provides a variety of fresh herbs and greens as well as flowers."

Octavia appeared with a basket of tiny cheese muffins to go with the salad.

"Next question – where did you manage to find such a talented couple?" Elaine wanted to know. "Octavia is such a terrific cook, and Esteban seems to do many things well."

"They've been with me for a number of years. I lived in Mexico for a time. When I moved back to the States, they came along. They live in the little house you might have noticed as you drove in."

"What about the rest of the ranch? You must need a large staff to run it when you're not here."

"It varies with the season. I have a ranch foreman who runs the actual farm operation with the help of however many he thinks he needs. They live in the bunkhouse. My ranch manager – the one who sent you the directions for finding the place," he smiled at Lisl, "oversees the whole thing. Pays the bills, all that sort of thing, and keeps in touch with me."

"Does he live here too?" Caro asked.

"No, he stays here occasionally, but he lives in town. He's young, and there certainly isn't much doing around here in the evenings to keep a young fellow interested."

Esteban brought the platter of meat to the buffet to carve while Octavia removed the salad plates and wine glasses to be replaced by red wine glasses. Then she brought the dinner plates.

"That smells wonderful," Lisl said.

Esteban added thin slices of meat to each dinner plate which already contained tiny puffs of potato along with baby carrots in an orange-honey glaze and crunchy pea pods.

Everyone oohed and aahed and ate with enthusiasm.

"The elk is really good," Jud commented with a note of surprise. "I wasn't sure how much I was going to like it."

"It's great," Doc agreed. "This sounds like a sizeable operation you have here. What kind of horses are you raising?"

"Oh, thoroughbreds, of course," in a voice that suggested there were no other kinds worth considering. "Kentucky isn't the only place good horses come from."

"And the llamas, are they just for fun, or are they profitable too?" Jud wanted to know.

"Mostly they're for fun although an income can be made from breeding. They make good pets, if you have the space, and excellent pack animals. And the market for their wool is increasing. Someday they may pay their way here, but I go along with Lisl. I have them mainly just because I like them."

Brant absorbed all the conversation as he enjoyed his dinner. The meal was great in spite of the gnawing thought that he was coming from way behind in trying to compete for Lisl with all this. Colman was suave, urbane, sophisticated, all the rest of the words like that he could think of. And obviously wealthy too.

"And what are all of you going to do for the rest of this holiday weekend?" Colman asked.

"When you're retired, holidays and weekends don't mean as much as they used to," Caro answered, "but we're all playing in the couples' golf tomorrow afternoon. And that makes me think – would you like to come and play too?"

Oh no, Brant thought. Caro, you and your big ideas. Don't invite him, but Caro was hurrying on.

"It's just a fun game for only nine holes, and then we have a pot-luck picnic at the river afterward."

"But you said it's couples," Colman protested. He turned to Lisl. "I suppose you're already spoken for?"

Caro answered for Lisl. "Yes, she and Brant are playing together, but we have room for one more couple, and I know a delightful widow who would love to play if she had a partner. You know, Linda Hampstead," and she turned to the others at the table. "Linda is a good golfer too."

"Sure, come on and join us," Jud backed up his wife. "It looks like the weather is going to hold for at least one more day. It's always a fun game, something like a two-ball foursome or a scramble, so there's no pressure. Our stakes are pretty high, though. Costs a dollar a person to get in the game, and sometimes we have to take up a collection of another dollar for charcoal for the barbecues."

"That's pretty high stakes," Colman laughed. "But I think my manager would allow it. That sounds like fun. I'd be delighted to join you if you're sure the lady is available."

"I'll check first thing in the morning and let you know," Caro assured him.

"And you said a pot-luck picnic," Colman went on. "What may I bring?"

"Whatever you want for meat to barbecue. A few people bring steaks, sometimes chicken, more often hamburgers or hot dogs. There's always so much food that you wouldn't go hungry if you didn't bring anything but your appetite."

"But I should contribute something to the festivities."

"Well, just bring some chips or some sort of nibbles for a little happy hour while we wait for the barbecues to get ready to cook. The first tee time is at one o'clock. I'll let you know when you're scheduled when I call you in the morning."

"I appreciate your including me. I was looking at a very quiet day. This will be a pleasant change of pace."

Octavia and Esteban removed the dinner plates and brought dessert, a smooth caramel custard with a raspberry sauce drizzled in a spiral pattern around it.

"That dinner was absolutely marvelous," Lisl said, "and the dessert is just right after a big meal."

Everyone agreed. Esteban poured coffee and passed a plate of chocolates.

"I need a chocolate like a I need a hole in the head," Doc said, "but I can't bring myself to pass it up."

That remark reminded Brant of the two killings. He'd forgotten them for awhile with the good dinner and interesting conversation. In fact, the dinner had been so great he was almost ready to like Colman. All the others seemed to. Must have been the wine that had mellowed him. To be honest with himself, the man actually was very personable, and maybe he really was just kind of lonely here at the ranch. The golf tomorrow would work out okay. Linda Hampstead was a very attractive early-fifties widow who just might do Brant a favor by moving Lisl off Colman's center stage.

"Let's have a second cup of coffee in the living room," Colman suggested.

A fire burned on the hearth to welcome them. Outside the night was black with only the faintest light still showing the outline of the mountains in the west.

Jud settled into one of the comfortable chairs in front of the fireplace. "This is the life," he sighed. "I feel so full and satisfied I may never move again."

"Would anyone care for an after-dinner drink?" Colman offered. "Brandy, kahlua, crème-de-menthe, drambuie, Irish cream?"

"Thanks anyway," Brant refused. "Since I'm the designated driver, I'd better pass on this one."

"I'd love an Irish cream," Angie said. "Like Lee said earlier, I don't need it, but I love it."

"Lee?" Colman questioned. "Oh, you mean Doc. I guess I'd never heard your real name. How about you? What will you have?"

"A drambuie would be nice. I'm not driving tonight."

Jud reluctantly passed since he was driving the other car, but the rest of the group indulged in one or another of the drinks offered.

"And when would you like to come for that horseback ride?" Colman asked Lisl. "I'll be away from Tuesday until the end of the week, but anytime the week after."

"I'd like to try it, but it's been so long since I did any riding that I don't have the proper clothes anymore. I still have my boots, I think."

"Don't give it a second thought," Colman assured her. "Jeans are what we use around here."

"Well, fine then. Why don't you call me when you get back, and we'll set a day. It will be fun to get back on a horse again. I hope you have a gentle one. I'm out of practice for handling one with too much spirit."

"I have just the right little mare for you," Colman reassured her. "That's all set then. I'll call you when I get back."

"Oh, I hate to move," Caro said, "but if I don't, I'm likely to fall asleep right here. This mad social life is almost too much for me. First, Sylvia and Gerald's party and now this lovely evening. But I do think it's time we should head for home. We have an hour drive."

Profuse thank yous and compliments accompanied their progress toward the front door. Caro promised again to call Colman next day about the golf. Esteban opened the door for them, and their host saw them to their cars after assuring them the gate at the end of the drive would be open for them.

As Brant backed the car around and headed down the hill, Lisl yawned. "What a fantastic evening! I've never seen a house I liked more. Everything was just right." Elaine and Phil agreed sleepily from the back seat.

Brant thought about when they got home and would Lisl ask him in, and would he accept if she did? Yes, he hoped she would, and yes, he would accept.

CHAPTER THIRTEEN

Monday Golf

The crowd of golfers milled around the Upper Course pro shop waiting for their tee times. Westons were in charge of the game this time, collecting the entry money and handing out the score cards.

"It's a best ball of the foursome this week," Jud explained. "The cards are already marked with the strokes you get."

"Oh, Linda," Caro said to the attractive blonde sitting next to her at one of the outdoor tables, "here comes Colman now. Here we are, Colman," and she waved.

"Linda, this is Colman Lewis. And this is Linda Hampstead," she told him.

Brant was standing not far away and thought he detected a pleasantly surprised smile on Colman's face as he greeted Linda. Maybe he hadn't expected someone quite as terrific. Linda's hazel eyes shone with pleasure also at finding her partner to be someone more than just acceptable. The dinner guests from last night all greeted Colman and found an opportunity to again thank him for the evening.

The starter called the first couples foursome to the tee. Lisl and Brant were in the second group playing with Sylvia and Gerald Peck.

As they waited their turn Lisl asked, "You've known Colman a long time?"

"Sylvia hasn't," Gerald answered, but I've known him since we were in college together at Berkeley."

"Sylvia had told us he had a beautiful house, and she certainly was right," and Lisl went on to tell Pecks about their dinner party last night.

"I assume, since we heard nothing about a wife, that he isn't married?"

"Not anymore," Gerald said. "He was for quite a few years, but somehow he and Marcy drifted apart. I think she found someone else who was at home more often. You know, Colman is away most of the time. And I don't think Marcy cared much for the ranch either. She's definitely a city girl, but they're still good friends."

"Did they have any children?"

"Yes, a son who's grown now and works with Colman. He's in charge of their business in Hong Kong."

"I've never been able to understand," Sylvia said, "how there can be so much money in importing a bunch of toys and clothes."

Gerald laughed. "The toys and stuff like that are the bread and butter of his business. The real money comes from the art objects much of which he tracks down personally. He has a fantastic head for what's good and what it will sell for."

"Well, he's certainly a charming person," Lisl said, "and obviously very successful. I hope he has a good time today with Linda. Oh, it's our turn to tee off," as the starter called their names.

Brant and Gerald teed off with good to excellent results, and then Brant turned his attention to enjoying watching Lisl swing her driver. Her white shorts and print golf shirt fit exactly right to show off her figure as she swung the club around. A distinct pleasure to watch.

"You'd be ready for the ladies' golf tour if you had more time to practice," he told her as they headed down the fairway.

"Thank you, but that's not likely to ever happen," she said. "I like to play, but I'm not too fond of practicing even if I had more time. For me, it's just a good excuse to get out in the fresh air with friends and enjoy the beautiful world."

"Great game," Lisl said to their partners as they finished the ninth hole. "I think we did quite well as a team. Everyone helped. What did we end up with?" she asked Brant who'd been keeping the score.

"Thirty-two," he said as he finished adding. "I don't think that'll win, but it's respectable. We'll see you at the picnic?" he asked Pecks.

"Oh, yes," they assured him, "see you at the river."

"Food goes on this table," Angie directed, "and find yourselves a place to eat," as the golfers arrived for their post-game barbecue. Lisl and Brant found an empty table, spread their cloth and pulled out their table settings. Brant poured glasses of white wine for each of them.

"We're over here," Lisl called to Pecks.

"May we join you?" George Shedd asked.

"Sure," Brant told him. "We have room for eight at the table. Who'd you play with?"

"Linda Hampstead and that new fellow, Colman Lewis.'"

Oh, shit, Brant thought to himself. Now we'll have them at this table too. Oh well, can't be helped now. They can sit at the other end of the table. Now, Brant, he could hear his mother saying when he was a boy. You're not being very kind. I'm sure that other boy is really very nice if you'd just give him a chance. And Brant had to admit in the back corner of his mind that his mother would have been right about Colman. He was very personable, and Brant couldn't find anything about him to dislike except that he just didn't really like him. It was only because of Lisl, or at least he couldn't think of any other reason. He shoved the whole idea back further in his mind, and determined to have fun.

Colman and Linda joined the group. Linda brought a big salad to put on the buffet table. Colman uncovered a platter he'd brought.

"Oh, yum," Lisl said. "I think I detect Octavia's hand in that. It looks wonderful. When Caro said to bring some nibbles, I think she meant a bag of potato chips. We weren't expecting gourmet hors d'oeuvres. What is it?"

"Some Mexican mixture with home-made tortilla chips. Octavia doesn't tell me what she puts in things, and I don't ask. I just eat and be glad. So help yourself."

"Come and share," Lisl invited everyone. "It's delicious. How was your golf game."

"Linda played beautifully, and the Shedds are both very good. Yours truly contributed a bit here and there. But who cares about the game? It's a great day to be out with good company just enjoying life. Anyway, to answer your question, I think we had a 31."

"You beat us by one stroke. You know, if you win, you have to be chairmen for the next time. That's the way this game works."

"Never fear," Colman said, "someone will beat us."

"The barbecues are ready to cook," Doc called.

The river sparkled in the afternoon sunshine as it rushed past the picnic ground.

"Aren't we lucky the weather has been so beautiful lately?" Lisl commented to Brant. "May is often so cold. This is paying us back for the extra-snowy winter we had."

"It's great while it lasts, but I don't think we've seen the last of the cold weather," Brant guessed.

The golfers filled their plates from the pot-luck table and took their meat from one of the barbecues. For a short while it was comparatively quiet while everyone ate. "Here come Westons," someone called. "What took you so long? We didn't leave much food for you." "Attention everyone," Jud yelled. "Now for the big pay-off. First the KP's. Mary Lou won the ladies' – four dollars for you," and he handed her an envelope, "and Steve Parks won the mens'. He was only a foot from the hole." Much applause from the crowd. "Lisl and Brant and the Pecks came in third with a 32 and each get one dollar."

"Well, we get our investment back at least," Gerald said.

"Shedds and Linda Hampstead and Colman Lewis came in second with a 31 and each get two dollars."

"If I could double my money on every investment," George Shedd commented, "I'd be a wealthy man."

"And our winners this week and chairmen for the next event in two weeks are Jensens and Hurleys with a fantastic 29. They each get five dollars." Loud applause all around.

"What a wonderful day this has been," Colman said. "I can't thank you all enough for inviting me to share in your fun. I'll look forward to seeing you again when I'm in the area. Thank you for a great game and a lovely afternoon, Linda."

Linda turned on her 100-watt smile. "You were a wonderful partner, and I've enjoyed the day ever so much. Let's do it again."

That's just fine, Brant thought. You two will make a great couple and leave Lisl for me.

CHAPTER FOURTEEN

Tuesday Night

Brant's prediction about not having seen the end of winter came true Tuesday morning. Fog hung over the golf course, and frost whitened all the bushes. Weather was quirky at this altitude. Brant was glad he wasn't planning to play golf. Tuesday was ladies' day, and he hoped the ladies all dressed warmly. They were going to need it.

After breakfast he called Hardin.

"Did you find out anything at Valent's house?"

"Not much. Another case of the wife not knowing anything about the family finances. She just took what money he gave her and kept her mouth shut. She said he'd had a phone call Saturday morning. She didn't know who and didn't pay much attention to what was said. Barney told her was going out to meet a buddy and would be back sometime, probably late afternoon. It was early enough when we got there that she hadn't begun to wonder where he was yet. He took his pick-up and drove off."

"Did you find his rifle?"

"No, not yet. Found his pick-up parked off the road on the way to where we found him. Rifle wasn't in the truck, and it wasn't at home either. His wife said he always took it with him."

"Looks like whoever shot him took the rifle too. To keep us from matching bullets. Does his wife know what kind he had?"

"She thinks it's a 30.06."

"That fits. Anything else?"

"Yes, a bank book. I wouldn't have been surprised if he kept his money in a coffee can buried in the back yard, but he had both checking and savings accounts at the local bank branch in Lakeside. Rose said he paid all the bills. There wasn't much in the checking account. The savings account showed deposits in December of a thousand dollars a couple of times. Nothing since. We'll try to follow up on his farm accounts, when he sold his crop or any beef and when he paid off any loans. I think those thousand dollar deposits look like payoffs rather than farm income."

"Seems likely. Did his boots match our casts? And the truck tires?"

"Yeah, sure did. So now we know Jacob and Barney were two of the poachers."

"What we really need is the third one. He must be the one who runs the show, this 'Jer' Barney mentioned. Anything from the P.O. box addressed to Jack Jones?"

"No, I didn't have much hope there. If it had been a box in Lakeside, we'd get something maybe, but Farwell is too big. No one remembers who rented the box. The bill for the box rental goes to the box. They don't have any other address."

"Have you had a chance to talk to any of Barney's friends yet?"

"Only his brother. He was at the house when we went to talk to the widow. He called his wife to come over and console Rose. She was pretty shook-up. We'll go back when she's had a chance to calm down."

"What about Barney's message for Grady Brown to meet him at the bar tonight. You still want me to keep that date?"

"You bet. Pretend you don't know anything about Barney's death, and see what develops. But tell me about your weekend. How was that big dinner party? What's the place like?"

"Pretty fabulous. It'd be hard to design a house that looked more at home on the land than that one. Colman must have had an excellent architect. It's a gentleman's hobby farm, but a working one too. He's raising thoroughbreds and llamas along with the alfalfa and hay to feed them. And he has a fair size staff, a Mexican couple who manage the house and cook and serve. They live there. Then there's the general manager who lives in Farwell, and a ranch overseer who lives at the ranch in a bunkhouse along with seasonal help."

"So how was the dinner, any good?"

"You may have guessed I'm not overly fond of Colman, but I have to be honest. It was one of the better meals I've ever had. Drinks and tidbits on the terrace watching the sun set on a gorgeous view of the mountains, the elk was barbecued with some marinade that was super, and everything that went with it was done to perfection. Couldn't quibble about a thing except that he monopolized Lisl's attention."

"Uh huh, and I'm understanding why you aren't too fond of the guy. Anything else interesting?"

"Yes, he has a mounted elk head that is one of the best and biggest I've ever seen. Boone and Crockett have rated it a 350. He said he shot it himself last fall. He never said if the elk we had for dinner was from the same animal. I doubt it. That head came from an old and tough specimen, would be my guess. I managed to be clumsy and stick my hand in the blood from the meat before it was cooked. Wiped it on my handkerchief. I'm thinking it might be worth a trip to Ashland to the forensic lab to see if that blood matches any of our samples from the elk kill.

"Umm, good idea. What are you thinking? That Lewis is tied up in this somehow?"

"I don't know what I have in mind exactly. Nothing definite yet. I guess I'm just curious."

"Can't hurt, might help. Want me to set it up?"

"Sure. Do you know the people there?"

"Yes, they've helped us out before although since they're federal, they don't get involved unless we run into something like you're talking about – DNA and that sort of thing. When do you want to go?"

"Sooner rather than later. I might as well make it tomorrow if you can set it up. Tell him I'll be there before noon."

"Will do. And I'll arrange with Tony Marcus to get the elk samples ready for you. Have a good time at Frank's tonight."

Brant drove up to Frank's Bar again. He recognized a couple of pick-ups in the blinking red neon. When he opened the door, the room was strangely quiet. Only eight men sat at the table in the corner, no other customers and no loud music.

"Howdy, Frank," he greeted the bartender. "Where is everybody? Had too much weekend?"

Frank looked at Brant for a long moment. "Guess you ain't heard. Barney got killed Saturday."

Brant feigned shock and disbelief. "You must be kiddin' me. Barney dead? But he left me a message. I was supposed to meet him here tonight. How could he be dead? He was fine last Friday. What happened – car accident?"

Frank hadn't taken his eyes off Brant's face. Brant had the feeling Frank was checking out the response to see if it rang true.

Kenny came over to the bar. "Come on, siddown, and we'll tell ya what we know. It ain't much."

Brant followed him over to the table shaking his head. "I can't believe it. Not Barney. So tell me about it, what ya know."

"Goddamn if he wasn't shot right through the back of his head. His brother, Will, - you remember him? – got it from the cops who came to tell Rose. Will happened t'be at Barney's house when the cops come. Rose said he got a phone call Saturday mornin' and went out an' that's the last she seen of 'im."

Brant shook his head again and ran his hand through his shock of hair. "I just don't get it. Who would wanna kill Barney? And I wonder how come he wanted me to meet him here tonight. What was he gonna tell me, huh? We were gonna do some huntin' together. Any you guys know what he was thinkin' about?" Brant looked around the table. He noticed Frank watching him from behind the bar.

None of the other men had any ideas about what Barney's plans might have been.

"Is there gonna be a funeral? Barney was nice to me. The least I can do is come an' tell 'im goodbye."

"Don't know yet. The cops have 'im now, and nobody knows when they'll let Rose have 'im. Will said the cops had a search warrant for the house. They took some things, and wanted to know where Barney kept his rifle. Rose said it was in his truck."

"And ya know what," Brant went on, "I bet the cops'll be around wantin' to talk to alla you guys. Somebody gets shot, they wanna know everythin' from everybody who ever knew the guy."

That started a babble of conversation while Brant listened. None of them seemed to know anything about the illegal hunts Barney had participated in last winter, and they made no connection between Jacob Kowalski's death and Barney's. No one mentioned a person named Jer nor any letters addressed to someone called Jack Jones. A picture began to come clear in Brant's mind. While the men rambled on, Frank stood silently at their end of the bar just listening.

After about an hour Brant said, "I guess there ain't much use me hangin' around. I'll never know what Barney wanted to see me about." He shook his head sadly again. "Now you be sure an' let me know when the funeral's gonna be, or if ya hear anythin' else I'd wanna know about."

Frank spoke up for the first time. "The rest of you guys get outa here too. I'm gonna close up. Don't feel like keepin' open tonight."

Brant was surprised, but no one else seemed offended that Frank didn't care if he threw out a few good customers. Everyone shuffled toward the door and out into the night. They called out goodbyes of "See ya later" and "We'll be in touch" as they climbed into their trucks. Frank had already shut the front door and turned out the lights.

Brant pulled out onto the highway headed toward Rivermount while the other trucks took side roads away from Lakeside. He glanced in the rear-view mirror as one more set of headlights came onto the highway. He was already far enough away that he couldn't be sure if the lights came from the Bar parking lot or had already been on the road.

There wasn't much traffic on a Tuesday night following a long weekend. Everyone was already at home. Far back Brant could see the high headlights of a semi and ahead of him the taillights of another, but that was all except for the one car behind him. Those lights stayed at the same distance mile after mile. As he neared the entrance to Rivermount, Brant made a decision and drove right on past toward Farwell.

On the outskirts of town he pulled into the big truck stop and went to a phone. The lights of the car following turned in also but drove to a shadowed area of the big parking lot. All Brant could tell about the vehicle was that it was a dark pick-up. He leafed through his billfold until he found Elsie Swenson's phone number. Grady Brown's landlady.

"Elsie, this is Grady Brown, your roomer, remember?"

"Oh yes, are you going to be home tonight? I was just about to lock up."

"As a matter of fact, that's exactly what I had in mind. I'll fill you in when I get there in about fifteen minutes. Leave the porch light on, okay?"

As he drove out of the parking lot Brant tried to watch for the dark pick-up, but other traffic got in the way. When he turned off the highway onto a side street, he drove slowly. Sure enough, a dark pick-up turned off too. If he'd wanted to, Brant could easily have shaken the tail. Instead, he was happy to have whoever it was see him go to Elsie's house.

He turned into the quiet street of '20s and '30s bungalows. A porch light gleamed at a neat white house on the left at the end of the block. Brant crossed into the driveway and went to the door. Elsie heard him and had it open for him.

"Hi, I'm Grady Brown," he told her.

"Well, now you just come right in," Elsie said as she closed the door behind him.

If ever I need to rent a room in someone's house, Brant thought, Elsie would be my ideal landlady. Her halo of snowy hair framed a sweet face with merry blue eyes above pink cheeks. She'd be hard pressed to stretch up to five feet two or tip the scales much over 100 pounds.

"Did you want to stay all night?" she asked.

"I'm not sure yet. I don't want to put you to any trouble. I can just snooze on the couch."

"Oh, nonsense. It's no trouble at all. The other bedroom is all made up waiting for you," and Elsie grinned... "Would you like a little glass of sherry? I like a bit myself, but I don't like to drink alone."

Brant returned her grin. It reminded him of his English mother who had enjoyed a wee tot of sherry before bed.

"Yes, that would be nice. Thank you."

Elsie went to the old-fashioned built-in buffet in her dining room and came back with two crystal sherry glasses on a small tray along with some cookies the English would have called biscuits. She handed one glass to Brant, left the tray and cookies on the table between them and settled herself in a comfortable chair with the other glass.

"Now tell me what brings you here tonight, Grady, or do you want to talk about it?"

"How much did Hardin tell you about me?"

"Only what I was supposed to tell anyone who came asking about you."

"Then, if it won't offend you, I think for now it's best to leave it that way. Then you won't make a mistake if someone comes again. What exactly did Barney ask about me when he was here?"

"Oh, just what you'd expect. Did you live here? I said you rented a room but didn't take your meals here. Were you home? No, you hadn't come home last night. I giggled and said I thought you had a girl friend and stayed at her house some nights. Where did she live? I told him I had no idea, that I didn't snoop in my roomer's affairs. Indignant, I was. Then he wanted to know if he could leave a message, and you know about that, I guess, since this is Tuesday night."

"Uh huh, Hardin gave me the message. I went to meet Barney tonight, but of course he wasn't there."

Elsie looked puzzled a moment, then understood. "That man who was found shot last weekend – his name was Barney, wasn't it? The same man?"

"Yes, and I'm here now because someone followed me after I left the bar."

Elsie looked properly shocked. "Whyever would anyone do that?"

"Just to be sure I'm who I say I am and live where I said. In a little while I'll check to see if he's still here. If he's gone, I won't need to stay overnight."

"Oh, my, this is all very puzzling but exciting too," and she picked up the knitting beside her chair.

"How did you become acquainted with Hardin?" Brant asked.

"Well, I've known him all his life. His folks and I were neighbors way back when he was a little lad. Once in awhile he asks me to help out like this with some small bit of business. He and his wife have me over for dinner now and then. I'm alone now. Harry died years ago, and the children don't live nearby. Hardin's a good man."

Brant agreed, finished his glass of sherry and then asked, "Is there a window where I can see the street without being seen?"

Elsie frowned and thought, "No, not very well." As with most bungalows like this one, the living and dining rooms went across the front of the house with the kitchen and bedrooms in back. The view of the street was cut off from those rooms by the neighbors' houses.

Then she amended her negative. "Oh, yes, you could now that I think about it. If you don't mind climbing up the attic stairs, there's a little half-moon window above the porch. Do you think that would do?"

"Worth a try. Just show me where."

Elsie took him to the central hallway of the house and showed him the stairway.

"I don't go up there very often. Too hard to climb the steps. You may run into some cobwebs."

"No problem. Turn out the hall light, please." Brant headed up and opened the door at the top of the stairs. As his eyes adjusted to the dim light coming in from outside, he could see the attic was full of assorted cartons and trunks, but there was a clear pathway to the little window. He shut the door and carefully felt his way. When he reached the window, he stood back from the glass and bent down to see out. Good, he had a clear view of the whole street. In the shadow of a large tree at the far end of the block he could just barely make out the dark shape of a pick-up parked at the curb.

He stumbled back to the door, slipped through and down the stairs.

"He's there. Now is there some way to get outside and along the street without being seen?"

"Hm, that's another problem. Let me think. You might be better off to go out my back door and around the block. That way whoever is in the car won't see you, and the neighbor's dog isn't so likely to bark."

Brant smiled. "You think of everything. Thanks."

Elsie showed him the back door and the pathway to the side street. Brant told her he'd come back in the same door in a few minutes.

As he made his way around the block, he was grateful for the big old trees in this neighborhood. He could keep in shadow easily until he came almost to the corner opposite where the pick-up was parked. He stepped behind a large shrub and peeked around it carefully. It was too dark to see anything inside the truck except a bulky shape. As he watched, the person shifted, moved around, then struck a match to light a cigarette. That was all Brant needed.

It confirmed what he had figured. Frank was the one who was in contact with the mysterious Jer or Jack Jones. As he retraced his way back to Elsie's house, he brought back in his mind his conversation with Barney at the bar last Friday. No one could have overheard them except Frank who could easily have stepped out into the back storeroom near the end of the bar. He was probably the one who had pointed the finger at Jacob Kowalski too. None of Barney's friends seemed to know about his illegal hunting deals. Jer had probably instructed him to recruit a stranger who wouldn't be missed if it became expedient to dispose of him. Now Barney himself with his big mouth was the disposable one.

Brant told Elsie he'd take her offer of a bed for the night. There was no way he could leave without alerting Frank.

When Brant woke from a refreshing sleep, Elsie was already up.

"I think your friend has gone," she told him. "When I brought the paper in, I didn't see any pick-up."

"Good. Then I'll get out of your hair, and I certainly thank you for being so hospitable."

"You'll stay and have breakfast, won't you? Or at least a cup of coffee," as Brant shook his head.

"Okay, a cup while I use your phone, if I may."

Hardin answered his office phone on the first ring.

"Good morning. This is Grady Brown calling from Elsie Swenson's excellent bed-and-breakfast."

"C'mon now, what kind of nonsense are you up to this early in the morning?"

"No kidding. When I left Frank's Bar last night, someone followed me. I decided I'd better come to my landlady's house."

"So give me the whole story. What happened down there last night? Were they surprised to see you?"

"Not much. I think I played my part pretty convincingly. Said I had a message from Barney to meet him there. Acted surprised and amazed and properly sad when they told me Barney had been shot. None of his friends seem to know anything about the illegal hunts. It looks like Barney was told to recruit some nobody to take part – someone who wouldn't be missed if they offed him."

"So who followed you?"

"That's what I mainly called to tell you. It was Frank. He must be the one who has blown the whistle on Kowalski and Barney when he thought they talked too much. So he knows who Jer is. Maybe you can lean on him when you're investigating Barney's death."

"I'll make me a little visit down south and see what I can come up with. How'd you and Elsie get along?"

"Just fine. If I didn't already have a place to live, I'd consider this one."

"Glad it worked out. She's a dear soul, a good friend. Where are you off to now?"

"I'm heading over to OSP to pick up those elk samples and take them down to Ashland. I'll be back tonight."

"Tony will be expecting you. I'll talk to you later."

In the small waiting room at the OSP Farwell headquarters, Brant told the officer on duty that Tony Marcus was expecting him and was buzzed through the admitting door. Tony came to meet him with the package of frozen elk samples.

"Thanks for your help," Brant told him, "and I wonder if you could do me another favor."

"Sure. What do you need?"

"Do you have a record of who got elk tags last fall?"

"Right in the computer. Who do you want to know about?"

"Colman Lewis. He has a whomping big elk head on his living room wall. Says he shot it last fall. I'm just curious."

Tony headed to a computer, punched a few buttons and watched the screen.

"No tag for that name. More than likely he bought it from someone else and was just telling a little white lie to impress you. We run into that quite often. He's that guy who bought the old Western Bar S ranch isn't he? From what I hear, money's no problem for him. Uh huh, and that's where you got the elk blood on your handkerchief? I'm beginning to get the picture. He probably bought the elk you had for dinner from the same source.

"Maybe that explains it, maybe not. We'll see what comes of this little jaunt of mine."

CHAPTER FIFTEEN

Wednesday

Following the directions he'd been given, Brant turned in at the sign reading National Fish and Wildlife Forensics Laboratory, Department of the Interior, Fish and Wildlife Service. The director came to greet him.

"Hi, I'm Clyde Bennett," he introduced himself as he shook hands with Brant. "You've brought us something?"

"Yes, as Metcalf told you on the phone, we're working on an elk poaching case which has involved two murders. I've brought samples of the elk that were killed along with some blood on a handkerchief. I'm hoping you can tell me if there's a match."

"Come on to the serology lab, and I'll get this started. Then we can tour the place. You've never been here before?"

"No, you were just getting into high gear about the time I retired, and the occasion to visit never came along. I've heard about the great things you've been doing, though."

Clyde turned the corner into a lab and introduced Brant to Dr. Mason Meinhold.

Mason is our head of serology," he said as he handed over the package Brant had brought and explained to the doctor what was needed.

"Are you in a desperate hurry for this?" the doctor asked.

"Not desperate," Brant smiled, "but sooner rather than later. We're not at a dead end yet. There are other threads to follow, but this would shed a whole new light on the investigation if the blood on the handkerchief happens to match one of the meat samples."

"We're kind of backed up right now, but we'll get the results to you as soon as possible."

"Thanks, Mason," Clyde said. "Now let me show you our establishment. This is morphology on the other side. Criminalistics are in another area. We have the latest in equipment for identifying species, determining the cause of death and connecting the suspect to the crime. It's a never-ending battle to try to save our dwindling wildlife everywhere. Samples come to us from all over the world."

Brant followed along as Clyde showed him one laboratory after another dedicated to cutting the ground out from under those who were preying on endangered species.

"I'm impressed more than I can say," Brant told the director. "I know these criminals are a wily crowd, but it looks to me as if you have the upper hand."

"I wish we did," Clyde said with regret. "What comes to our attention is a drop in the bucket. We can't hope to cover all the borders and entry points in the country. So much slips past us. And then there are the cases like yours right here in our own backyard. Come on out to our warehouse, and I'll show you what I mean."

Brant gazed in amazement at the huge room with row after row of shelves stacked floor to ceiling with confiscated illegal goods. Stuffed animals, turtle shells, ivory, elephant hides and artifacts, furs, boots and purses of reptile skins, tourist souvenirs, feathers, all made from parts of creatures it is illegal to use. Some of the articles were good quality, but many were tacky or utterly gross. Brant couldn't imagine how anyone would want to walk down the street wearing a pair of boots made of cobra skins with the heads of the cobras on the instep. Or what woman would want a purse made of caiman skin with the head of the caiman on the flap of the purse.

"Your lab is very encouraging, making me think we're going to get ahead of the poachers," he told Clyde, "until I see all this. It's totally depressing," and he shook his head.

"I know," Clyde agreed. "All we can do is keep plugging away. We have some brilliant people working here. I like to think we're gaining on it. Are you staying over to go to one of the plays?"

The small town of Ashland in the southwestern corner of the state was more famous for the Oregon Shakespeare Festival than for the forensic laboratory even though the lab was the only one of its kind.

"Not this time," Brant said. "We'll be back later in the summer after the outdoor theater opens." The Festival complex contained an Elizabethan style theater open only from mid-June until fall as well as two indoor theaters which rotated plays through most of the year.

Clyde showed Brant to the door. "We'll get your results to you very shortly. I hope we can help."

"Thanks, it's been an education to see the place."

Brant glanced at the gas gauge as he approached Lakeside on his way home. Oh-oh, getting kind of low. Probably about enough to get back to Rivermount, but I might as well stop here and get some. No use worrying about coasting home on the fumes.

He pulled into a station and told the attendant to fill it up. He'd just handed over his credit card when he saw the proprietor of Frank's Bar come around the corner of the building.

"Well, howdy, Grady. Didn't expect ta see ya again so soon. Where ya been?"

"Just out for a drive." Brant thought fast. "Went over toward summa those lakes down Crater Lake way. Thought I'd see if I could find me some deer or elk even if poor old Barney ain't around any more to go huntin' with. How 'bout you? You like to hunt?"

"Some." Frank wasn't any more chatty than he'd ever been.

The station attendant brought Brant's credit card back for his signature. Frank leaned toward the car while Brant wrote on the charge slip.

"Well, now that's interestin'," he said. "You changed your name or somethin'?" That don't look like Grady Brown to me."

"I've got charge cards for a coupla names," Brant answered. "Handy for emergencies, y'know. Don't worry," he said to the attendant who was looking alarmed, "it's legal. See, signature matches the one on the back."

Don't sound quite right ta me," Frank said. "You got the law after ya or what?"

"Well now, I wouldn't say that exactly." Brant made his voice sound casual. "Let's just say I'm takin' a new road lately."

"Lemme look at that," and Frank grabbed the charge slip from the attendant. "Brant Grayson, huh. I'll remember that name in case I meet ya somewhere else."

Brant put his credit card back in his pocket and started the engine.

 . "Sure thing, Frank," he said. "Be seein' ya," as he drove back onto the highway. Damn, I couldn't have asked for worse luck. Grady Brown will have to leave town for good now. He was useful for awhile, but not any longer. I don't like Frank knowing Grady and Brant Grayson are one and the same. If he gets word of that to Jer, it leaves me in a very exposed position. A line of worry creased Brant's forehead.

Friday

Thursday morning Brant called Hardin to tell him about the encounter with Frank.

"Brant, how're you doing?" Hardin answered the phone.

"Okay, but I thought I'd better tell you that Grady Brown has gone south forever."

"Now what?"

"I stopped for gas in Lakeside yesterday on my way home from Ashland, and who should come up just as I was signing the credit card slip but dear old Frank. He made a point of reading the name on the card, and he didn't swallow my lame story about having two different cards. Now he knows Grady and Grayson are the same person, and I have a hunch it won't be long before Jer, or whoever he is, knows too. I'm not overjoyed about that prospect. I doubt I'm likely to be on his list of favorite people."

"Oh hell," Hardin exclaimed. "I don't like it either, but I'm not sure just what we can do about it unless you want to leave town until this is over."

"No, nothing like that. We'll just wait and see what develops. We'll be in touch," and he hung up.

Then he phoned Lisl.

"Can you get off tomorrow long enough for a golf game?" he asked.

"I'd love to, Brant, but Colman called and I'm going riding with him."

"Oh." Brant felt all the joy go out of life. "I thought he was out of town."

"He came back sooner than he'd expected, and since it looks like it will be a nice day, it seemed like a good idea."

"Hey, you never had said you liked riding until lately. We could have gone anytime here. I used to be a cowboy, you know. Worked on my uncle's ranch all through school before I went in the Navy."

"I guess the subject never came up before. Let's see how I get along this time, and then maybe we'll try it together. Thanks for inviting me to play golf, and I'll take a rain check if I may."

"Sure, well, I guess I'll go up Paulina-way and see how much snow is left to get in the way of the fishing season. Have a good time, but keep your eyes open."

"Just what is that supposed to mean?" Lisl's voice turned frosty.

Brant wished he hadn't started this, but he couldn't quit now. "Just that I don't think everything Colman's told us is true," he finished lamely. He didn't want to tell her about the elk head – what he'd found out about it – yet.

"Brant, I've had the feeling all along that you don't really like Colman, and I think that's very unkind of you." Lisl's voice sounded distinctly cool. "He's been nothing but charming to all of us, hospitable and friendly. I suppose being suspicious of people comes from your job, but I find it upsetting."

"I'm sorry. Didn't mean to upset you. Sure, he's a nice guy." Brant fumbled for words to undo the damage. "Have fun, and I'll see you later."

Fog closed the world into a woolly pocket Friday morning. Brant had his breakfast, read the paper, then did some cleaning around the house and put a load of clothes in the washer. He'd learned in the last two years how much Ann had done to keep their home orderly. By the time he'd finished the chores, the gray blanket of fog had thinned, and the sun finally shone through. Time to pick up his mail and then head out of town.

As he drove the road up to the lakes in the caldera of an old volcano, he thought about his relationship with Lisl. She had moved into a prominent place in his life. Was he in love with her? He didn't know – guessed it was moving in that direction. Was she in love with him? After yesterday's conversation, probably not, he had to admit. Was he unduly suspicious of people? He didn't think so. Lisl had no understanding of what it meant to be a policeman's wife.

Ann had learned about what it was like to be married to someone in law enforcement as the years of their marriage went along. Brant knew she had been anxious for him many times, but she never complained about the odd hours nor the fact that he frequently didn't or couldn't tell her exactly what he was working on. Somehow, in spite of her own fears, she had managed to keep their two children from being fearful, and, bless her, she'd also managed to keep them from being resentful when he missed their games or recitals or whatever. Not every policeman is fortunate enough to have such a loving and understanding wife, and Brant would always be grateful for the life he shared with her.

Now he had retired, and he shouldn't any longer be living and thinking like a policeman, he told himself. Lisl shouldn't need to make allowances for him. How was it that he seemed to still keep getting involved? Was it true, once a policeman, always a policeman? Deep in his nature did he miss the excitement of the chase?

He enjoyed retirement immensely, the freedom to do what he wanted when he wanted. He was lonely for Ann, but he'd made many good friends at Rivermount, and until he stick his foot in his mouth yesterday, he'd thought Lisl might move into the void Ann had left. With luck, perhaps he could repair the damage.

His mind had been so occupied as he drove that he hadn't noticed any cars around him. There weren't many. Snow was still piled in patches along the road and a few deep drifts in the shade as he climbed higher. On a sudden whim he decided to drive to the top of the peak, what was left of the ancient volcano rim. He turned onto the gravel road leading up the mountain. As he wound upward the valley and Cascade Mountains opened out in breathtaking splendor above the remaining wisps of fog. Magnificent view, he thought as he rounded a curve and checked his rear view mirror. He was surprised to see another car coming behind him.

There was still some snow on the road as he gained elevation. Slushy and slippery in the sun. The car in back drew closer – a white pick-up. Brant could hear the throaty roar of the engine accelerating. He looked in the mirror again. The guy was in a hurry considering the condition of the road with the slush on it. Brant snatched quick glimpses in the mirror as he tried to keep his eye on the road. His cop's mind said he should give the fellow a citation for tailgating and driving too fast for the road conditions. He could see a bulky shape with a brush-top cut of light hair, but that was all.

The pick-up came closer, and Brant looked for a place to turn out and let him pass. Now it was so close he could see a grin on the man's face. No place to pull over. Brant speeded up as much as he dared, but the truck hung right on his bumper.

The guy's a maniac, Brant thought as fear made his stomach flop and his heart pound. Omigod! He's trying to ram me. The truck touched Brant's car causing it to slew sideways. Brant wrestled the wheel and brought it back under control only to have the truck ram him again, harder this time. He fought the panic that threatened to overwhelm him.

His rear wheels skidded toward the edge of the road. Brant struggled with the steering wheel to get his car back straight just in time to have the truck hit him full force sending him soaring out into empty space like an airplane without wings.

Rocks and trees rushed up to meet him as his car landed with a crunching thud. In spite of his seat belt Brant felt the instant pain of breaking bones. Blood trickled into his dry mouth when he licked his lips. His heart thumped inside his ribs as he fumbled to release the belt and open the door. Had to get out, he thought. Car might catch fire.

He looked back up the hillside and saw a hefty man standing on the rim with a rifle at his shoulder aimed at Brant. The noise of the gun exploded over the mountains and reverberated ominously. Brant cowered down in the seat as he heard the bullet thud into the car's interior somewhere. Whoever it was wanted to make sure Brant didn't live any longer. Another shot hit the rear of the car, and Brant smelled gasoline. His assailant intended to set the car on fire.

Brant shoved with his feet and found his legs didn't hurt. With all the energy he could muster, he slid himself over to the passenger side, away from the man above him. He found his right arm would work as he tried to open the door. It stuck. The frame of the car was sprung holding the door shut. He was vaguely aware of the roar of the truck engine racing back down the mountain road. The effort to move was too much for him. Blackness closed in.

"Easy does it, Brant. We'll get you out of here." A voice spoke soothingly.

Brant struggled to open his eyes. A face swam into view. Now the car door was open, and his savior was trying to get him out. Brant sucked in his breath with a gasp as he tried to move. Something was very wrong with his body. It hurt fearfully.

"It's me, Brant, Tony. Can you help me get you out? The helicopter will be here soon to take you to the hospital."

"Glad you're here," Brant struggled to say, but the words didn't sound right. Breathing was painful, and something else hurt like hell.

"Come on now," Tony urged. "Slide over here."

Brant shoved with his feet against the car floor and managed to get himself closer to the open door. Tony reached to try to lift him, and Brant screamed.

"Sorry, won't do that again," Tony soothed. He folded Brant's left arm carefully across his body, then worked his own arms under Brant. "Now push with your legs."

Brant pushed as hard as he could while Tony lifted him out of the car and helped him to lie down on a thermal blanket in a patch of snow. Brant could still smell gasoline, and wondered vaguely why there wasn't any fire. The sound of a helicopter engine drifted over the trees, and he let the darkness swallow him up again.

Soft footsteps intruded into his sleep, and he opened his eyes. The sun shone in a window on his bed and assorted bits and pieces of hospital gear. The footsteps came to his side accompanied by a round face with a cheerful smile and snapping blue eyes.

"Good morning. Welcome back to the world of the living. How are we feeling today? A little stiff, maybe."

Brant wondered why nurses always seemed to use the "We" pronoun. "I don't feel much of anything. Am I alive?"

"Just barely. You've been shot so full of pain killers it may take you awhile to come to. But there's nothing wrong that time won't cure."

Brant closed his eyes again. Breathing was difficult, and keeping his eyes open was such hard work. He reached out his left hand, and the searing pain immediately stopped that movement. He wanted to know what was wrong with him, what had happened, what day it was. Before he could manage to put his questions into words, he fell asleep.

Any sense of time vanished into a deep void as he slept, woke and was vaguely aware of people around doing things to him, changing IV's, carefully shifting his position, checking his temperature and blood pressure, emptying the bag from the catheter, lifting the covers to give him another shot of something. Soft footsteps and soft voices, gentle fingers prodding, and then he slept some more.

CHAPTER SEVENTEEN

Sunday

Sunlight woke him again, really woke him this time. He swam to the surface of consciousness and opened his eyes without difficulty this time. He suddenly felt hungry. How long had it been since breakfast Friday?

He tried taking a deep breath and decided immediately to settle for little breaths. Same with the left hand. Yikes, why did it hurt so much? Carefully he lifted the hand only from the elbow down, not moving the upper arm. Nothing wrong with that. The problem was up higher.

Blue eyes and round smiling face came in the door. Her name tag read "Ellymae".

"I see you've returned to us again. How're we doing today?" she said as she checked his blood pressure.

"Better, I think. And when do we eat around here?"

"Oh, you are better, aren't you? Tired of nothing but an I-V. Well, your own doctor is on his way down the hall right now, and he'll decide if you're ready for a steak or Jello. Now let's get your temperature," and she stuck the thermometer under his arm for a few moments.

"You don't stick it in my mouth anymore?'

"New inventions all the time," she assured him. "If you haven't been in a hospital for awhile, you'll be amazed."

Dr. David Walden shoved the door open.

"Glad to have you back among us," he said. "I thought for awhile you were going to sleep all week." He looked over the chart at the end of the bed.

"Dave, how come you're here? How did you know I needed you?"

"The hospital staff found my name on your file when they brought you into Emergency."

"Can you give me a fast rundown of what's been going on in my little world? Last I remember I was flying in a car, not an airplane, and I seem to recall landing with a whump."

"That you did, and you're lucky Tony Marcus happened along to pick up the pieces. You have an assortment of cracked or broken ribs, a broken left clavicle, and a nasty bump on your head plus multiple abrasions. You aren't going to feel like anything very strenuous for about ten days, and I'm not going to want you trying to do much for six weeks."

"Six weeks! The summer golf season will be half over."

"I can see where your priorities lie."

"For now my priorities lie with getting something to eat. It's been a long time since breakfast."

"Just which breakfast did you mean?"

"Well, uh, this morning - ? No? I guess not, since I guess it's morning now. Yesterday? What day is it anyhow?"

"Sunday."

"Sunday! You mean I lost a whole day and two nights? No wonder I'm hungry."

"I'll see you get something, a soft diet for an empty stomach today. Maybe something better tomorrow."

"I'll stay long enough to get something to eat, and then I'm going home," Brant said. "I've got things to do."

"One day at a time for now. We'll get you up on your feet and see how it goes. Can't let you go home until you can manage by yourself unless you want a nurse coming in."

"I'll manage just fine."

"Sure," the doctor said. He'd heard that story before from guys who thought they could handle the world.

Ellymae took over when Doctor Walden departed.

"I'll crank your bed up, and then we'll put you on your feet. Now hold your left arm across your chest and ease your legs over the edge. Use your right hand on my shoulder to steady yourself. There you go, good."

The broken and cracked ribs explained his difficulty breathing, and the broken collarbone kept the left arm from functioning like it should. Ellymae steadied him as he put his feet on the floor.

"Okay now, easy does it, right this way to the bathroom."

The first steps were tentative, but he felt stronger with each one. When he had finished in the toilet, Ellymae instructed him to sit in a chair while she changed his bed. Then she brought a table with washing utensils and told him to get washed for breakfast. He looked in the mirror and recoiled in horror.

"Yuck, how'd I get to look so awful?" There was a large bruise on his forehead, and both eyes sported shiners. A scab had formed on the crook of his nose, broken years ago, but it didn't look any more misaligned than it had.

"You took quite a bump. It'll all heal, though. You'll be back to your usual lovely self before long."

"I'll have to put a sack over my head meanwhile," he said as he gingerly washed around the sores.

"Now let's get back in bed for breakfast," Ellymae told him. She helped him negotiate the maneuver and get his long legs folded back under the blanket. The exertion tired him enough to make him doze off.

He woke to the sound of dishes rattling on the breakfast cart in the hallway. A perky nurse's aide shoved the door open and set his tray on the swinging table in front of him. Eagerly he took the covers off the dishes and drank the glass of apple juice while he surveyed the rest of it. A bowl of oatmeal with brown sugar and a plate of scrambled eggs with a muffin. Not much for a Sunday breakfast.

"Where's the bacon or sausage to go with the eggs?"

"You're kidding of course," Ellymae said as she finished straightening his room. "You're on a soft diet, you know. So eat and be glad of what you have," as she went out the door.

Brant put milk on his oatmeal and tried it. Good enough. He tried the eggs too before they got cold. They were okay. The muffin was fine if you liked muffins. He'd rather have had something good in the way of toast. Anyway, it was all okay, and he ate with appetite for a few minutes until suddenly he felt full and too tired to eat anymore. He leaned back against the pillows. Maybe the doctor was right. He wasn't ready to go home yet.

The breakfast tray was gone, and he had dozed a little more when he heard a soft knock on the door. His daughter, Marty, peeked in.

"You're awake and feeling better, I can tell," she said as she came over to the bed to give him a kiss.

"Marty, it's good to see you. How did you know where to find me?"

Marty taught high school English in the small town east of Farwell. Brant never tired of her cheerful smile and the lovely face that reminded him of Ann. Not that she looked just like her mother. Her eyes were blue and her hair sandy like his. But there was something of Ann, the way she looked at him. She was five feet four and slim, a satisfying specimen with a personality to match. Brant had a sneaking hunch Bill Wilson, the football coach at the high school, thought so too.

"Doctor Walden called me Friday night. Bill brought me over, but you were totally out of it. I guess you didn't know I was here?"

Brant sighed. "No, I sure didn't. I'm pretty vague on a lot of what went on. What did the doctor tell you?"

"Just that you'd been hurt in an auto accident up at Paulina and had to be brought in by Air Life. He said you were banged up with some broken bones but nothing life threatening. I'm glad you're feeling better. I was kind of worried Friday night. The doctor said there wasn't any point in my coming again yesterday, that you were still out but that you'd probably be awake by today. So here I am."

"How about your brother? Does he know about this?"

"Yes, I called Cory and Melissa. The doctor didn't think there was any need for them to drive over from Portland, but I'll call them again and let them know you're coming along okay."

"Good, so how's everything with you?" Brant switched the conversation away from himself. "School okay?"

"Thank heaven it's nearly over for the semester. When it gets close to the end of the year, the kids get so antsy it's hard to pin them down to concentrate on anything."

"And what about summer – what're you going to do?"

"I'm teaching summer school for six weeks and then working at a camp for underprivileged children. That'll give me two or three weeks for some R & R before it starts all over again. Here, I brought you a book, Tony Hillerman's latest. I read it – really good."

They chatted on companionably. She knew he liked mystery stories, Hillerman's especially. Brant often felt he didn't see enough of his children considering that they didn't live too far away, but they were busy with their own lives. It was nice having a quiet time to talk with Marty, but after awhile his eyes tended to droop shut.

"You're getting tired," Marty observed. "I'll let you get a nap. Do you want anything?"

Brant smiled. She was always a perceptive child, aware of other's feelings. "Thanks no, I don't know if I need anything or not. But come again if you have time, or phone. And thanks for coming. Tell Bill it was nice of him to bring you the other night."

"Bye for now then," and she kissed him gently. He watched her leave and felt the deep love of a parent for his child.

Marty was the first of what turned out to be a steady procession of visitors. Brant had time to close his eyes a few minutes before Angie and Doc Michaels arrived.

"Well, hi," Angie said. "What are you doing to yourself? You look like you tangled with a chain saw."

"How'd you know where to find me?" Brant asked.

"It's in the paper this morning. Headlines and everything. Rivermount resident brought by Air Life to hospital. Injured in accident on Paulina Road."

"No kidding. What else did it say?"

"Not much, really," Doc answered. "Whoever is in charge is playing it close to the vest. Nothing detailed about your injuries or how it happened. Said you skidded off the road which was slippery from slush. Car was airborne and landed in a drift of snow, or it would have been much worse. Said the snow kept the car from catching fire."

Brant could remember now wondering about that. As Doc talked, more of his memory returned.

"Now tell me what's hurting besides the obvious bump on you head?" Doc asked.

"My ribs are sprung, and the collarbone is broken. I'm afraid I won't be able to win the club golf championship this year like I was planning. And I had such high hopes," he said chuckling. He was a middling good golfer with no real hope of winning any championship.

"Uh huh, that clavicle will hold you back for awhile. It's one of the more painful fractures. How'd it happen?"

"I'm more than a little hazy about it. I remember driving up to see how much snow there still was. I decided to go up to the top. Part way up the road got slushy, and from there, I don't remember very well. A pick-up came up behind me, and I think it ran into me which is what pushed me over the edge. I'm just not sure, but it'll come back to me."

"Everyone is worried about you," Angie told him. "Of course it happened too late on Friday to be in that day's paper, and it wasn't on the evening news either. We weren't home last night for the news so we didn't know anything about you until this morning. How long will you be here? Can we get you anything? Do you need clothes?" Angie went right to the practical matters.

"I'd like to go home today, but the doctor isn't agreeable. Maybe tomorrow. He says I have to be able to take care of myself which may not be too easy with one arm. As far as clothes are concerned, I haven't any idea what happened to those I had on. I'll have to find out. Otherwise I can't think of anything I need. Marty was here and brought me a book. A good drink of scotch would go down nicely, but I doubt that's on the menu here. What's doing around home, anything interesting since I left? I feel like I've been gone forever."

"We went out to dinner last night with Jud and Caro and to the community theater for a play so they hadn't heard about you until this morning either. They'll be in to see you sometime today. I feel terrible that you've been lying here since Friday, and none of us even knew."

"Don't worry about that," Brant reassured her. "From what I'm told, I was out of the picture until today."

The perky nurse's aide came bustling through the door bearing a cheerful bouquet of early spring flowers.

"How lovely," Angie said as she handed Brant the card. "Who's it from? Or am I being nosy?"

Brant read the card, "As ever, Lisl". He wasn't sure exactly what that meant.

"Lisl," he told Angie.

"She'll be in to see you later too, I know. I talked to her this morning. She was frantic when she saw the news. I think that girl cares more than a little for you."

Brant couldn't help smiling happily, not that Lisl was worried but that she cared. The memory of their last conversation which hadn't been exactly friendly came back to him. Maybe her day with Colman hadn't worked out too well, he uncharitably hoped.

"We'll leave you to get a little rest," Doc said. "If it turns out you're doomed to be here awhile, I'll see what I can do about the scotch. Nothing like treating another doctor's patient. Take care now, and mind the nurses."

"See you at home soon, Brant, and tell the doctor you have lots of friends who will help you," Angie said.

"Thanks for coming, and I'll let you know when I'm ready to leave. We'll have a coming out party."

As Michaels headed out the door, they literally ran into Westons arriving. The noise level in the room rose many decibels with greetings to each other and to Brant. Finally Angie and Doc left and Westons settled down for the usual questions about what happened.

"I brought you a tape player and some nice music tapes," Caro told him. "It will put you in a relaxed mood to ease the hurt. We're all just so concerned and sorry for you. Now when you come home, you're not to worry about a thing. You won't need to cook or clean or anything. And if you have a hard time getting dressed, Jud'll come over and help you, won't you dear?"

"You're great to offer," Brant replied, "and don't think I won't take you up on it. With that kind of help, the doctor just might let me out of here maybe even tomorrow."

The rattle of the lunch carts signaled food time again.

"Oh, it's time for your lunch," Caro said. "We'll leave, but let us know when you want to go home, and we'll come and get you and bring you whatever you need in clothes."

Brant felt weary from all the chatter but warmed by the obvious caring and willing helpfulness of his friends.

The lunch was about what he'd expected for a soft diet – mashed potatoes and gravy with some sort of minced meat, overdone carrots, pudding. He was tired enough that he didn't feel as hungry as he'd expected.

Ellymae came in, surveyed his lunch tray and told him he'd have to eat more than that or the doctor would never let him go home. She handed him another pain pill, plumped up his pillows and pushed the button to lower his bed.

"I'll do better next time," he promised her and closed his eyes again.

The bustle of visitors passing in the hallway woke him. He looked at the clock and realized he'd been asleep for over an hour. Ellymae came in again.

"How about getting up and sitting in the chair for awhile. You need to get yourself vertical now and then."

It felt good to get on his feet and move around. That little nap was what he'd needed. Ellymae settled him in a reasonable looking robe to cover the hospital gown, put a blanket over his knees and handed him his book. He hadn't progressed past the title page when Campbells arrived with Lisl.

"Brant," Lisl exclaimed, "you look awful."

"Thanks a heap."

"Oh, I didn't mean it that way," she hastened to amend. "It's just that you look so hurt. I'm so sorry."

She reached for his left hand but drew back quickly when he told her "Not that one, this one," and extended his right hand. She pulled over a chair and sat down close to him.

"You did yourself in right properly," Phil commented. "Give us the story."

And Brant went through what he knew again. It was so incomplete. When he had time and energy later today or tomorrow he'd have to call Tony or Hardin and try to find out what had really happened to him.

He wished Lisl had come by herself. With Campbells here he couldn't say all that he wanted. In fact, the whole conversation was trivialities. He thanked her for the flowers but didn't want to ask about her day with Colman, and she didn't mention it. Time for that when he felt more able to cope with the previous unpleasantness.

"We brought you the paper," Elaine said. "We thought you might like to see your name in print."

"I'd rather it had been for a hole-in-one or something important like that, but thanks for thinking of it."

"We mustn't stay too long and wear you out," Lisl said after a half hour of chatting. She rose, leaned over to give him a kiss and whispered "Love you" in his ear. As they went out the door she turned and looked back with a small frown making lines between her eyebrows.

He watched them out the door, his eyes lingering on her attractive figure in tailored slacks and knit shirt that all fit just exactly right. But the frown didn't fit – she should be smiling her usual sunny smile. She'd said Love you, but maybe that was just an easy remark, and he was still in the doghouse.

Ellymae came back in the room and told him they would just have time for her to take him on a walk around the halls before her shift ended. She handed him a cane, "just in case", and he shuffled out and around the circle of hallway past the doors of other patients, some with visitors, some looking very ill and alone. He felt lucky not to be one of those.

"Back to bed for awhile now," the nurse told him. "I'll see you tomorrow. Don't give the night shift a bad time and eat your dinner, you hear?"

CHAPTER EIGHTEEN

Fear

Brant put on one of the tapes Caro had brought. The music flowed around him in an easy rhythm, and he closed his eyes. He had every intention of getting into his new book, but instead he dozed again. He didn't know how long he'd been asleep when something woke him. He looked at the open door and saw a man built along the lines of an old-growth tree trunk standing there looking at him, a man with a brush cut of light hair topping a head that sat squarely on his shoulders. He wore jeans and a western style shirt with fringe and embroidery. His boots attracted Brant's attention – cowboy boots of cobra skin with the heads of the cobras on the instep.

Fear prickled up Brant's spine and caused his stomach to jump. He didn't know the man, and yet he did. Their eyes locked, and Brant heard the echo of a gun blasting the mountain silence. He saw the malevolent grin on the man's face reflected in his rear-view mirror just before the crash.

"Next time," the man said in a surprisingly high voice from such a big body, and he moved out of sight.

Brant lay motionless, paralyzed from the evil he felt. Something corrupt. When he could force himself to move, he pushed the blankets off, swung his legs out and shuffled to the window. Visitors were leaving in the late afternoon sunshine, moving toward the cars in the parking lot. In a few minutes Brant saw the man emerge from under the hospital portico, and sure enough, he headed for a white dual-wheel pick-up. As he had his hand on the truck door, he turned and looked up at the rows of windows. Brant stepped back from the glass. He knew he probably could be seen, and he had an overwhelming desire to hide.

The truck drove out of the parking lot, and Brant sat down on the bed. His legs shook. It wasn't easy to get himself back under the blankets. No part of his body seemed to work right including his heart which banged noisily in his chest.

The door opened, and a cheerful man entered whose name tag said he was Jim. He introduced himself as the evening shift nurse and proceeded to take Brant's blood pressure.

"Whoa," he said as he watched the scale. "Have you been up and dancing around too much? Your pressure is jumping off the scale."

Brant wanted to say he'd had a major scare, but how could he explain? It wouldn't make sense to tell someone a man standing in his doorway had given him a fright. He passed it off with platitudes.

"Take it easy for awhile. Supper will be along soon," Jim told him.

By the time the meal carts rattled in the hall again, Brant had managed to calm his heart and stop the flip-flops in his stomach. The supper looked more appetizing than lunch had, a tasty soup and macaroni and cheese which turned out to be surprisingly good for institutional cookery. A dish of applesauce and a sugar cookie completed the menu. In spite of his fright he ate it all. That should give him a gold star on his chart.

He turned over in his mind who this man was and why his appearance had set Brant's heart to pounding. For sure he was the driver of the pick-up that had rammed Brant and caused him to be here in the hospital. And the dual-wheels on the pick-up sent a message. Also the cowboy boots.

Could he be the third member of the elk poaching ring? But why was he so threatening to Brant? Nothing had ever been said publicly about Brant helping with the investigation. Had Frank already let this person know that Grady Brown and Brant Grayson were the same person?

Another knock on the half-open door and Tony Marcus came in.

"Tony, you're just the man I want to see," Brant said. "Come in. I have so many questions, and something to tell you too."

"Good to see you up and in the same world with the rest of us. You were off in outer space for awhile. I'm just on my way home from work and thought I'd check on you."

"I guess thanks are in order to you for finding me. How come you knew where to look?"

"It was just luck, coincidence. I was parked up the road a little way beyond the turn-off to the peak. I'd just finished some business with a Forest Service friend when I thought I saw your car turn up the hill. Then not far behind I saw this white dualy follow you. I was just curious enough to fall in at the end of the procession. I kept far enough back that the dualy couldn't see me. There aren't any turn-offs on that road so I knew I couldn't lose him. When I heard the rifle shots, I speeded up. Before I got to where you'd gone over the edge, the guy came zooming back down so fast he nearly crowded me off the road."

"Did you get the license number?"

"No, he went by too fast. I could have followed him down, but I wanted to find you. I figured you were the object of the shots. I radioed for anyone to keep an eye out for the truck, but he must have taken back roads. No one saw him."

"So we've lost him again," Brant sighed with disappointment.

"Not entirely," Tony reassured him. "While you've been lying here idly, we've been busy," he teased. "Everyone on the force has been asking around about that truck – at gas stations and car dealers and anyone else who might give us a line on him. We matched the tire tracks and the boot prints in the mud where he stood to shoot at you with the ones we had before. So now we know he's the third man on the elk party and almost certainly he's the one who killed Barney and Jacob. We found one of the bullets he shot at you – lodged in your car – and it matches too."

"And you know who he is?"

"We got his name from the dealer who sold him the truck last summer. I knew it was a new model. His name is Jack Jones, and we got his address too. Unfortunately that didn't help us much. It's a little house on a back street. No one was home, and according to the neighbors, he's rarely there. They say he drives a white dualy, but no one has seen him since early spring. His mail comes to a P.O. box in Farwell. Hardin says you've already checked that out, and it's a dead end. None of the neighbors have ever talked to him. What few times he's been there, he's not been the chatty type."

"And that's where it stands?" Brant frowned as he thought about it. "He has to live somewhere else, not necessarily close by. I'd guess Jack Jones is an alias, and the house is just so he'll have an address whenever it's required. Did you get a search warrant for it?"

"Not yet. We haven't decided whether we want to let him know we're onto him."

"I think you can quit worrying about that," Brant said. "He was here about an hour ago."

"Here! Did you talk to him? How do you know it's the same guy?"

"Believe me, I know. I'm not likely to forget that face in my rear-view mirror. No, I didn't talk to him. I was so startled to see him, I was paralyzed. I was dozing and opened my eyes to see him standing there in the doorway looking at me. He just grinned this nasty smile at me and said 'next time' and walked away. I watched out the window and saw him get into the white dualy. I don't mind telling you it shook me up."

Tony was thoughtful. "I guess it wouldn't have been hard for him to find you since your name was in the paper this morning with enough details of the accident for him to know it was you. And then he could get your room number here easily."

"You know about my little charade that Hardin cooked up, Grady Brown visiting Frank's Bar in Lakeside?" Tony nodded. "Grady is gone for good now," and he told Tony about his meeting with Frank at the service station.

"I've decided Frank is the tie-in from the bar to Jones. He must have let Jones know my name and also that Barney was talking too much. But Barney told me the man's name was Jer, that Jack Jones was just a name on the P.O. box as a contact. Which means we really don't know who he is yet."

"And how did he know you'd be on the road to Paulina last Friday?" Tony wondered. The two men mulled it over a few minutes to no avail.

Then Brant asked, "Back to the accident, how did you know where to find me?"

"It was easy to see from the tracks where you went over the edge. We've had a big share of good luck in parts of this investigation, and that was another one. He missed you when he shot at you, and his shot to the gas tank didn't set the car on fire since it was mired pretty deep in an old snow drift. And the snow cushioned your impact, or you might have been banged up a lot worse. I'm sorry to say that you're in the market for a new car now. The old one is headed for the junk heap after we finish going over it. It wasn't easy to get it out of the rocks, but now it's been towed in to our lot."

"I was beginning to think I needed a new one anyhow," Brant said. "We've had good luck and bad luck. Good that circumstances kept some things from being worse, and bad that so far we've run into dead ends. Maybe Hardin can get something out of Frank if he leans on him. I'm sure Frank knows who Jack Jones really is since he was able to get a message to him more quickly than writing to the P.O. box like Barney did. Barney was dead next day after he shot off his mouth to me."

"It may seem like a dead end, but we're putting the pieces together. Now you know what he looks like so give me a description."

"He's built like a brick outhouse, about six feet tall, brush cut light hair, no neck, mean round face, mean toothy smile, wearing western clothes, good quality, not shabby, and cowboy boots of cobra skin with the heads on the instep. I saw some like them at the forensic lab in Ashland. Illegal besides being gross. And wait a minute – something just popped into my memory. I saw him fire at me, and he shoots left-handed. Now you know what he looks like and his truck too. Shouldn't be too hard to spot him."

"We'll get his description out. Already have the truck on our list. Hardin and I have kept in touch so he knows what's been going on. How're you feeling, incidentally? We've been so busy tracking crime, I forgot to ask. When they brought you in Friday afternoon, you were out of it, and that's what they told me yesterday too."

"I'll be honest – a few things hurt like hell, the broken collarbone and ribs. I'm eternally grateful that you came along and rescued me so quickly. I could have been lying there for days. That road isn't much traveled this time of year."

"I'm glad I was there too, for you and also to get a line on that truck. Don't be discouraged – we're making progress. We'll get him. Now I better be going on home before my wife puts out a missing person report on me. See you later."

After Tony left, Brant lay thinking about the whole case. He tried to call Hardin, but there wasn't any answer. Sunday night, of course. He was probably out somewhere enjoying a respite from the world of crime. The evening shift nurse came in with another pain pill and helped Brant get settled for the night.

CHAPTER NINETEEN

Monday

When Dr. Walden made his rounds Monday morning, he found Brant awake and eager to go home.

"This looks to me like a good day to get out of here," Brant told him.

"Sure, why not," the doctor agreed after consulting the patient's chart. "You're going to have to take it easy, no heavy lifting. Give those bones a chance to mend. I'd say you can do what you feel like doing because you're not going to feel like much for awhile. I'll want to see you next Monday. By then the bones should be getting together again. Just don't push it, and you'll be fine."

Ellymae came in, and Dr. Walden told her he was sending Brant home.

"Just when we get to be friends, he sends you away," she told Brant. "That's how it goes."

"What happened to my clothes?" Brant asked.

"Here in the closet in a bag. They aren't in very good shape. I don't think you'll want to wear them."

She opened the closet door and took out what little was there.

"The pants look more or less okay," she said as she looked over the garments. "They're kind of dirty, but that'll wash out. The shirt had to be cut off you. The jacket is wrinkled but not damaged."

"I wasn't wearing it. It was on the back of the seat beside me."

Ellymae held up the jacket. "But there's a hole in it. I don't know if it can be mended. Look," and she showed it to Brant.

"That's a bullet hole."

She was aghast. Her blue eyes opened wide.

"A bullet hole! Who was shooting at you? I thought you were in a car accident, ran off the road on ice."

"It's a long story that isn't finished yet." Brant fingered the hole in the jacket. "Damn, that turkey came a little too close for comfort. And ruined a good jacket."

"And I have a feeling you're not going to tell me your long story," Ellymae said as she turned to the dresser and pulled out a plastic bag. "That's okay. I'll find out someday. Anyway, here's your wallet and watch and keys. Your shoes and socks are in the closet too, muddy but wearable."

"I'll call a friend and have him bring some clothes. What time do you want me out of here?"

"Before noon if possible. Have your breakfast, call your friend and that should be just right."

Brant had finished breakfast when Hardin shoved the door open.

"How're you doing? I hope you feel better than you look. A couple of beautiful shiners you have there, and your nose doesn't look so good either."

"I'm getting too old for this kind of caper," Brant sighed. "I don't heal quite as fast as I used to. You didn't tell me Grady was in mortal danger. Look at this jacket, just look at that hole."

Hardin looked stricken. "Guess we should have figured it might get dicey for you. Someone's done in two people already, what's another more or less. I heard the details of your accident from Tony, but he didn't mention the bullet hole in your jacket. How'd that happen without killing you?"

"I wasn't wearing it. It was over the back of the seat beside me. I didn't know about it last night when Tony was here – just discovered it this morning when I asked the nurse where my clothes were. I remember seeing the guy fire at me, and I slid down as far as I could go. He may have thought he hit me. He fired again at the gas tank and then left in a hurry. Maybe he heard Tony coming."

"At least we know the truck now, and everyone and his dog are looking for it. Tony said the same Jack Jones was the owner's name which must be an alias. But we'll get him sooner or later."

"Sooner, I hope. He was here yesterday and threatened me, said 'next time'."

"Here! How come I didn't know that?"

"Tony stopped last night on his way home from work, and I told him – gave him a description. Everyone should have it by this morning. I tried to call you, but you were out."

"I wonder how he found you. And does he know you and Grady are the same person?"

"I'm sure Frank is the snitch who put the finger on Jacob and Barney, and since he knows I have another name besides Grady Brown, he probably told Jer or Jones. Did you go have a chat with Frank yet?"

"Yeah, but I didn't find out much. I threw the name Jack Jones at him, and it shook him for a minute, but he denied knowing anything about him. Didn't know anything about what happened to Kowalski or who might have blasted Barney. As you've noticed, he's not very talkative. Your name didn't come up, but of course, that was before you ran into him at the gas station."

"Now Grady Brown has taken off from around here, never more to be seen. Say, I just remembered – have you heard back from the forensic lab yet? Or has Tony? That was last Wednesday, and they said it wouldn't take long."

"Haven't heard yet. I'll check with Tony. Maybe it'll come in today," Hardin said.

"If that DNA matches, it gives us a whole new line to follow. Maybe Lewis's only connection is that he bought the meat and head from our perp, but just maybe he might know something more. And for sure Frank knows who the guy is. I don't think the rest of the gang at the tavern know much. Barney must have had his instructions to rope in some transient who wouldn't be missed if they removed him, and Grady was next in line. Barney wouldn't have wanted to get any of his relatives or friends into the mess."

"Well, Grady did a good job for us while he lasted. Without him we'd be nowhere, but it's for sure he's left town." Hardin frowned. "I don't like the fact that Jones knows who you really are now. It won't be hard for him to find out where you live either. When're you going home?"

"Today, just as soon as I can get someone to bring me some clean clothes."

"I'm not happy about that. You'll be a sitting duck – house full of windows, no neighbors close. How about staying with someone else until we catch this guy/"

"That could be awhile. I hate to impose on my friends like that," Brant said.

"Hell, what are friends for. You know as well as I do that any of 'em would be glad to have you. When you wear out your welcome one place, you can move to another. In fact that could be a very good idea. Keep the bad guy from getting a fix on you."

"Ah jeez, Hardin, I'd rather be home. I'm not going to be very good company for awhile. The gang will be in and out to help, I know. I don't want to ask them to do more."

Hardin scowled and shook his head. "Stubborn old ox. If that jerk takes another shot at you, don't say I didn't warn you."

"Thanks for thinking about it. I'll be careful."

"And I'll tell the security force at Rivermount to keep an eye on your place whether you like it or not. I'll be going now." He hesitated at the door. "Sorry it turned out like this. You weren't supposed to end up as a target."

Brant called Westons, told them where to find a key hidden outside his house, and where to look for the clothes he needed to come home. Within an hour they were at his bedside. Ellymae helped him wriggle gingerly into a shirt.

"It'll be awhile before you're going to want a shirt or sweater that goes over your head," she told him, and Brant could tell she was right. No way could he get his left arm up in the air enough to put on a slipover garment. Since he'd retired, he wore knit golf shirts most of the time. He'd have to rummage around in his closet to find more of the old business shirts he still had.

Home never looked better as Westons turned into his driveway. Caro took charge, as Brant knew she would.

"Now you just come in and sit down wherever you're the most comfortable," she told him, "and I'll get some lunch ready. And I'll open up your bed for when you want to get in it. Angie and Doc are bringing your dinner tonight, and Campbells tomorrow. I called Lisl too, and she said she'd stop by at lunch time."

Brant smiled gently to himself. He'd known Caro would have her humanitarian aid all organized. Jud hovered around wanting to help Brant get settled in his big chair. His face grimaced in sympathy as his friend grunted trying to get comfortable.

Lisl came as Caro dished up the soup and sandwiches for lunch.

"I'm so glad you're home," she said. "I hated seeing your house dark and lonely these last nights. Now I want to know just what this was all about. I have a feeling this is more than just an accident."

Brant took a bite of his sandwich which gave him time while he chewed to decide how much to tell them.

"It all goes back to the hike and the dead elk and the man's body we found. We found out who he was, a transient from California. In his pocket there was a match folder from Frank's Bar down in Lakeside – you know the place?"

"I've seen it on the highway, but we've never been in it," Jud said.

"It's a local hangout – not exactly the sort of place where you'd be likely to go. Anyway, Hardin came up with the idea that I could go down there and pose as a transient and see what I might find out. So I did, and I guess I stirred up a hornet's nest. The man who was found shot about a week ago out in the woods – it was in the paper last Sunday – well, he was the second one who was on that elk hunt. The third one killed him as well as the transient we found. And it was the third one who rammed my car and ran me off the road Friday. We've come to a screeching halt since it turns out the name we found for him is an alias. He's still out there, and until we find out who he really is, we're up the creek without a paddle."

"How do you know he's the one?" Caro asked.

"The bullets he fired at me match what we had before, and so do the tire and boot tracks."

"Bullets he fired at you? Oh, Brant," Lisl was horrified. "I don't like the thought of somebody shooting at you. And if he's still out there, what if he tries again? You're not safe, and I'm worried silly."

Brant smiled. "I'm glad you care, but don't worry. It's not the first time someone has taken a shot at me. I'll be okay."

"I'm not convinced," Lisl said, "but I have to get back to work. I'll look in on you later. I can't help but worry. Don't stand in front of the windows, and don't answer the door unless you know who it is," she told him.

"Yes, Mother," Brant laughed.

"You can laugh, but you know I'm right. 'Bye for now, but I'll be back."

"I don't know, Brant" Jud said. "Lisl is right. Maybe you should come and stay with us for awhile."

Brant didn't want to tell them that was exactly Hardin's advice. He was glad to be home in his own house, and looked forward to a nap in his own bed.

"Now you really don't need to worry. I'll be fine. I'll pull the shades at night. Thanks for caring about me, and thanks for the offer of staying with you, but it isn't necessary."

Caro looked as dubious as Lisl had. "I wish I was as sure as you seem to be. But for now, I think you ought to get some rest. I'll clean up the kitchen, and Jud can help you get to bed. Then we'll leave you in peace and quiet for awhile. You have a phone by your bed, don't you?"

"Yes, I have the portable one I'll take in the bedroom."

"Good. Angie and Doc will be over around four so you'll know when to expect them. Otherwise just ignore the doorbell, okay?"

"Sure," Brant agreed. He really did feel much safer with all this help. "Thanks loads for all you're doing. The lunch sure beat what I'd have had at the hospital or what I'd have fixed myself."

He was sleeping soundly when the ringing phone woke him. It took a few moments for him to swim to the surface of consciousness. The bell rang again and again as he fumbled for the damn thing.

Finally "Hello."

Nothing.

"Hello?" he said again.

No answer, but he could tell someone was on the line. The hell with you he thought as he punched the off button and lay back on his pillow. His ribs hurt from the effort of reaching for the phone, his collarbone hurt, and he realized his heart was thudding inside his bruised chest.

He's already found where I am. Brant could see that evil smile saying "next time". Slowly the pounding of his heart edged back toward normal. Maybe I should go stay somewhere else. No point in being foolish. I'll wait and see what Michaels think when they get here.

The phone rang again.

"Hello."

"Soon," that odd high voice said, and the line went dead.

An icicle of fear went down Brant's spine. This was someone acquainted with guns and violence and not averse to killing a man. On the other hand, what could he do in the daytime in Rivermount? The summer tourist season wasn't in full swing yet, but still, there were plenty of people around. Golfers came by regularly on the Upper Course, and bicyclers were all over the bike paths.

The daytime didn't present a problem. Night was something else again. A man with a rifle could find endless places to hide among the trees and bushes, a rifle with a telescopic sight. In the village center people were around in the evening, but in the residential areas once darkness came, quiet came too. A few people might be out walking, and the occasional raucous party could break the stillness. Otherwise, from about ten or eleven o'clock the area belonged to the various wild creatures – the deer, raccoons, coyotes, porcupines.

Brant looked at the clock. Nearly time for Michaels to come. Laboriously he levered himself up out of bed, struggled into his slacks, shoved his feet into slippers and shuffled out to the living room. As he went by, he unlocked the front door so he wouldn't have to get out of his chair to let Angie and Doc in when they came. The thought crossed his mind that maybe it wasn't a good idea to leave it unlocked.

Oh hell, what can happen in the daytime, he decided as he settled himself in his big chair. He swiveled it around to watch the golfers and realized he made a tempting target in the windows surrounding the room on most of three sides.

He couldn't help scanning the area around his house. He'd always felt absolutely safe here. So different from the city where he'd spent his working life. Now he felt the need to be wary, and he resented that. Anger at the man with the brush haircut and evil smile welled up inside him. How dare he intrude his lawless ways into a peaceful little village. Rage replaced fear in Brant's mind. This monster isn't going to drive me from my home.

"Come in," he yelled when the doorbell rang. What if it isn't Angie and Doc he thought as his heart jumped.

"We're here, your dinner detail," Angie called as she and Doc came in bearing dishes and baskets. I'm getting paranoid, Brant though to himself as he greeted them.

"Let me just put things in the fridge and turn the oven on low for this casserole. Then we're going to sit down and find out what this is all about. You've recovered your memory of the accident, I hope."

Doc came over to sit by Brant while Angie rattled pans and dishes around in the kitchen.

"How're you feeling? Still pretty sore?"

"Yeah," Brant acknowledged. "Dr. Walden wants to see me next Monday. I guess he thinks nothing is likely to improve much before then."

"Bones take about ten days, give or take a bit, before they patch themselves together again. And six weeks before you're considered healthy. This is a crummy way to louse up your summer just when the golf season gets really moving."

Angie came from the kitchen. "Okay, here I am ready to sit down and get the story, so tell us what happened."

Brant went over his tale again. Should have had them all here at once, he thought. Campbells'll want to hear it tomorrow night.

"Listen, someone's at the door," Angie said and stood up to go to the front hall.

"Don't open it until you know who it is," Brant said before he thought. Angie looked startled.

"Who're you expecting, for heaven's sake? The bad guys?" as she flung the door open to admit Elaine and Phil.

"We're bringing dinner tomorrow night," Elaine said, "but we couldn't wait to see how you're doing. I'd say you look better than you did yesterday, even with the black eyes. They aren't so black – sort of green now."

"We really came to get the low-down on what this is all about," Phil said.

"We've just been hearing it," Angie told them, "and it sounds like a cops and robbers thriller. Good grief, Brant, did you have things like this happening to you all the years you were a policeman? Last winter you got banged up on our ski trip murder, and now someone is trying to shoot you. And you're supposed to be retired."

Brant's managed a lopsided grin. "Isn't retirement great? So peaceful and quiet. Well, it was like this – ," and he went through the story again for Campbells.

"So you knew who the guy was who got shot last week," Phil said. "You were being kind of cagey about it."

"Yes, I went with Hardin to check it out," Brant admitted. "When you asked me about it, we were on our way to the party at Colman's, and I didn't want to put a damper on the evening by talking about another murder. I'd have told you who he was the next time I had a chance, and now you know."

"You must know at least a little about what this man looks like," Doc said.

"Yes, he's built like a Mack truck, has a brush haircut, light color hair, and a mean grin. And we know he drives a dual-wheel, late model, white pick-up. If you see anyone around who answers that description, run the other direction and call the cops."

The friends chatted for nearly an hour until the dinner in the oven began to smell delicious.

"Come on, Phil," Elaine said. "we'll be back tomorrow night. Have a nice evening, and you be careful, Brant. You're not a cat with nine lives, you know."

Campbells had no sooner departed when Lisl arrived. As always, Brant felt cheered just seeing her.

"Stay for dinner," Angie told her. "There's plenty."

"I'd love to," Lisl accepted. "It smells marvelous. Let me help you."

"Oh, it's not done yet. We're just getting ready for happy hour. Come on, Lee, it's your turn to get busy."

Doc took drink orders while Angie set out a tray with dip and vegetables.

"I always salve my conscience about eating all these nibbles by telling myself the veggies are good for me," she said as she passed the tray while Doc handed the drinks around.

"And now we're going to talk about something more pleasant than guns and killing and bad people," Lisl said. Her eyes reflected the green outside the windows as she looked at Brant with a mixture of worry and affection.

Brant settled himself again in his comfortable chair after dinner.

"That was a wonderful meal, Angie. You ladies are the best cooks ever," and he yawned. "'Scuse me. Guess it's getting toward my bedtime."

"We'll be glad to help you get settled for the night," Angie told him.

"Oh, that's okay," Brant said. "I'll rest here for awhile and let the dinner digest."

"Can we take you home, Lisl?" Doc asked.

"No thanks, I have my car here. I'll be along pretty soon."

"I don't like you out alone," Doc objected, "after dark and maybe with someone dangerous out there. Better come when we do."

"Oh, I'll be fine," Lisl said, and Angie kicked Doc's foot none too gently.

"Come on, Lee, help me carry things out to the car. I think Lisl and Brant have things to talk about."

"Huh? Oh, well, sure," Doc agreed as he noted Angie's meaningfully raised eyebrow.

Thanks and goodbyes were said, and Lisl returned from seeing Michaels out the door in the last of the evening light.

"Now," she told Brant, "we're going to close the shades, lock the doors, batten down the hatches and whatever else we can think of to make this house impervious to nasty intruders."

Brant pushed himself out of his chair and moved to the sofa while Lisl busied herself closing shades in the living and dining rooms.

"What about the kitchen window?" she called. "Don't you have a shade on it?"

"No, I never got around to getting one. Never seemed very important. It'll be okay."

"Now," Brant said and held out his good hand, "come and sit by me. I've been wanting to give you a kiss all day – for quite a few days actually. It's been too long."

Lisl didn't wait for a second invitation. She curled easily into the curve of his arm. Brant angered her when he worried her, but her positive feelings about him outweighed the negative.

"I don't want to hurt you," she said. "Let me know if I do."

"I won't even notice it," Brant assured her. "It's so good to have you here with me again," and he rubbed his cheek over her soft hair. "You're going to stay all night aren't you?"

"If you want me to. Yes, I think I'd better. You need a guard."

"I don't think I'm in condition to romp around very energetically. Will you mind if we don't?"

"Of course not, there'll be other days."

They sat in companionable silence for awhile, now and then sipping the last of the after-dinner coffee. Brant yawned again and then apologized.

"No reflection on the company, you understand. I think my body is telling me something."

"I'll just put these cups in the dishwasher and turn it on, and we'll get you to bed."

Brant followed her to the kitchen and reached for a drink of water. Lisl leaned over to open the dishwasher, and Brant moved out of her way just as an explosion shattered the kitchen window. Hot metal seared the side of his head as Lisl screamed.

"Brant, you're bleeding, oh, God, don't die."

"Get down from the window, and call 9-1-1," he mumbled as his legs turned to jelly. Slowly he slid down the face of the cabinets until he sat on the floor. Echoes of the shot, breaking glass, Lisl screaming, reverberated in his ears. He heard her talking on the phone.

"Oh, please come quickly, send the police, he's been shot. It's ten Mountain Lane. Yes, we need an ambulance too. He's bleeding. Hurry, don't let him die."

She hung up the phone and crawled over to Brant sobbing. Before she had time to do more than worry about him, there were footsteps on the porch.

"Be sure you know who it is before you open the door," Brant cautioned. His mind functioned on automatic.

"I can see the flashing lights," Lisl said. "It's the police."

"That was fast," Brant mumbled to himself as the Rivermount security officer came into the kitchen.

"I wasn't far away," he told them. "Hardin Metcalf at the sheriff's office asked us to keep an eye on this house. I can see why he was concerned."

"Did you see the guy? Driving a white dualy?"

"No, didn't see anyone. Looks like it came from the rocks and trees beyond the next lot. He probably parked on the next street over across the golf course. Easy to shoot, get across and be on another street and out of here. I'll put the word out to be looking for him."

The sound of a siren came over the hill, and the ambulance turned in the driveway.

"Brant, man, you're playing with a rough crowd," the paramedic said as he examined the wound.

"Hi, Russ, glad you're here. This is going to cut into my golf game, isn't it?" Brant had played with Russ, one of the village emergency medical technicians.

Lisl hovered over Brant. "Be careful with him," she cautioned. "He has broken ribs and collarbone already, before this happened."

"Somebody doesn't like you," Russ said as he cleaned the blood away on Brant's head. "There, now that doesn't look so bad. You're incredibly lucky, old chap. Another inch and you'd have cashed in your chips. As it is, you just have a crease in your scalp. But you'll have to go to the hospital. Any gunshot wound, y'know."

"Brant, you're coming back to my house," Lisl told him. "I'm not letting you stay here another minute. I'll come with you to the hospital and then see to it that you get settled safely."

The security officer came back in the house. "We'd like to stay here and look around while you're gone. I'll lock up when we finish. I've called Hardin, and he'll meet you at the hospital. Take care."

"Thanks," Brant smiled wanly.

Lisl followed him out the door. Another trip to an emergency room. Twenty years had gone by since her divorce, since her too-frequent hospital visits with her former husband, and here she was doing it again. But somehow this seemed different. Brant wasn't getting himself hurt willfully doing dangerous things just for the thrill of it. Did that make her anxiety any less? No, but it put a different spin on it. She'd get it straight in her mind later. For now, all that mattered was to have him recover and then keep out of any more trouble.

CHAPTER TWENTY

Tuesday

Hardin waited in the Emergency Center as the Rivermount ambulance pulled in.

"Can't you keep out of trouble?" he joked. "Just get you out of here this morning and now you're back. Let the meds get you in hand, and then you can tell me all about it. Or Lisl can."

"Oh, Hardin, it was awful." Lisl's eyes brimmed with tears, and her voice had a note of panic. "We closed the shades in most of the house, but Brant doesn't have one on the kitchen window. Whoever it was waited there and shot right through the glass. We were there only a minute before he shot. What are we going to do?" Her voice came close to hysteria.

The emergency nurse worked on Brant's wound. He felt too tired to talk. His head throbbed, his ribs ached, his collarbone complained with a stab if he moved just wrong. He listened with only half an ear as Hardin talked.

"While you were on the way here, your security department called and said they'd had a report from neighbors across the fairway. They noticed a small dark car parked alongside the road over there. Didn't think much about it at first. They heard the shot, though and could see the flashing lights on the cars at your place. They looked out the window in time to see a heavyset man jump in the car and drive off in a huge hurry. It was too dark to get any description of him or the license of the car. The way those streets run, by parking over on that side of the golf course, he was in an entirely different area than your house, and he had a faster route out to the highway. I'd bet my last dollar it's the same guy, but he isn't driving a white dualy anymore. We'll be able to get the bullet out of your kitchen and tomorrow in the daylight maybe we'll be lucky and find the casing too."

Brant barely heard what Hardin was saying. His eyes drifted shut. Lisl took his good hand and kissed him gently. "We'll go home now to my house."

Dreams of war and battles and police chases and ambushes disturbed his sleep. By morning he felt wrung out and exhausted instead of rested. No position felt comfortable. Everything hurt. He stretched out his hand and found Lisl beside him.

"You've had a hard night," she said sympathetically. "I could tell you were fighting all night long."

"Sorry if I kept you awake."

"Not to worry. I'll make some coffee, and maybe that'll help you feel human again."

Brant struggled out to the kitchen and eased himself into a chair by the table. Some sips of coffee helped. Lisl busied herself at the stove, and in a few minutes put a plate of scrambled eggs in front of him.

"Here's some toast, and I'll warm up the coffee. Eat, and you'll get some strength."

She was right. The food tasted good, and the coffee woke him up. The side of his head felt funny when he chewed, but the throbbing ache had eased.

"Go make yourself comfortable wherever you feel best," Lisl told him, "while I clean up here."

Brant settled himself in the only chair Lisl had that accommodated his long legs. With his head back and his feet on a hassock he drifted between sleep and waking. As long as he didn't move abruptly or breathe deeply, he could keep his multiple hurts from tuning up.

The phone rang, and fear hit his stomach again. Then he remembered he wasn't in his own house. Jack Jones, or whatever his name was, wouldn't be likely to know he was here at Lisl's house.

"Hi, Hardin, you're out early," Lisl said. "I think he's better. He didn't sleep too well, but he ate his breakfast. It's been a really bad patch for him since last Friday. Do you have any new hopes of catching that awful man?" She listened for a minute, then "Good, I'll let you talk to him. Hold on."

"Here," she said as she brought her portable phone to Brant. "Hardin wants to talk to you. He has an idea."

"I'm here, Hardin, what's doing?"

"Glad you're maybe feeling a little better. I have the report from the forensic lab. They were all apologies for taking so long. It got buried on someone's desk. Anyway, we may have something. The blood from your handkerchief matched one of the elk samples, not one of the four you found, but one of those other three."

"That raises a couple of possibilities."

"Sure does. Either Lewis bought the meat and the head from our perp without knowing they were acquired illegally, or he's mixed up in it with both feet and knows very well where the stuff came from. I think it's search warrant time."

"Let me think about it for awhile, and I'll call you back."

"You got an idea?"

"Maybe," and he put the phone aside.

"What did he have to say?" Lisl asked. "Is he on the trail of the bad guy?"

"He got a report back from the forensic lab which may open up a new line for us. But never mind about that right now. Just come and rest with me awhile. It looks like a lovely day. Are you going to the office?"

"Yes, later. They can get along without me for now."

"Tell me about your day horseback riding last week. I haven't had enough chance to talk to you since then. Did you have a good time?"

"Yes, it was lovely. I haven't said anything because I had the feeling you weren't interested or weren't too happy with my going."

"Sorry I was churlish. Just jealous, I guess."

Lisl smiled. "You don't have to be jealous. Colman is very nice, but he's no competition for you. Anyway, it was a pleasant day. I went late in the morning. The little mare he had picked out for me was a sweetie. Plenty of spirit but not headstrong. We rode out around the fields and then into the woods and up to a fabulous view spot with a panorama of the mountains down by Crater Lake all the way north to Mt. Hood. Absolutely gorgeous."

"It's a pretty spectacular country we live in."

"Aren't we lucky? We stopped and had a little picnic that Octavia had packed and just admired the scenery. Before we went out, he showed me around the barns and introduced me to the workmen and showed me more of the horses. There are two Mexicans who don't speak much English and the foreman, Jerome. Colman has some beautiful horses. Some he has raised himself, and some he's boarding and training for other people. One horse is huge. I've never seen a bigger one except for draft horses. That one belongs to Jerome who looks kind of tough, but he was very polite."

Brant frowned. "What time was that?"

"Oh, I don't know, probably about eleven. I didn't look. Why?"

"Was the foreman there all the time?"

"No, he drove away while we were getting ready to ride."

"Did you by any chance happen to talk about me before he went away?"

Lisl thought a moment. "Yes, as a matter of fact, we did. Colman asked how all of our friends were – Westons and Michaels and Campbells and you. I said everyone was fine and that you planned to go up to Paulina that day and see if the snow has melted enough yet and how the fishing prospects look."

"What kind of car does Jerome drive?"

"A big white pick-up." Now it was Lisl's turn to frown. "Why all the questions? You look angry. What's wrong?"

Brant ignored her questions to ask another.

"Lisl, what does this Jerome look like?"

The urgency in his voice puzzled her. "He's solid, about six feet tall, the kind who'd need a horse that big, has very light hair in a brush cut. Tell me, Brant, why are you looking that way?"

"Lisl, that's the man who rammed my car over the cliff and shot at me. And I think he's the one who killed that transient at the elk mess we found and killed another man too. You say his name is Jerome. 'Jer' is all I had heard before, but your description, the big horse and the white pick-up – it all fits. Was it a dual-wheel truck?"

"Dual-wheel? Yes I think it was. I really didn't notice except that it seemed bigger than most pick-ups.

Now that I think about it, the back fenders stuck out sort of, and I think there were two wheels on each side. Is that the 'doolie' you've been talking about? I never heard the word before. Oh Brant, I can't believe he's the one."

"There's something else I'll tell you, and then I have to call Hardin. What he told me this morning is that our report from the forensic lab confirms that the elk we had for dinner at Colman's house came from one of those illegal kills we found. Also the mounted head he said he shot last fall - he didn't have an elk permit. Either he shot it without a permit, or he bought it from someone else."

"Brant, what are you telling me?" Lisl's voice sounded pained. "Are you saying Colman served us elk that was shot illegally and lied about the elk head? I can't believe he'd do such a thing. And he has a man working for him who shot at you?"

"Do you know where Colman and Jerome are now?"

"Colman is out of the country, I'm not sure where. I have no idea about Jerome. He lives at the bunkhouse on the ranch. I suppose he's there."

Brant reached for the phone and called Hardin.

"I've found out a few things to help you when you get that search warrant. Jer is Jerome, Lewis's ranch foreman. He lives at the ranch, but Lewis is out of the country now. When you go out, take someone who speaks Spanish. Some of the help don't speak much English. And keep me posted."

"Thanks for the leads. How'd you find out who he is?"

"Lisl told me she'd met him. The big horse and the white dualy are there too."

"I'll get busy with getting the search warrant. Do you want to come along? It'd be helpful since you've been there. That's if you feel up to it."

Brant hesitated. He was tired, but he hated to miss out as they closed in on their quarry.

"How soon would it be? And how would I get there? I don't have a car anymore, you know, and I couldn't drive it very well anyway."

"That's no problem. I'll send someone out to pick you up. But I need your input before I fill out the warrant form. How many buildings are there and how many people?"

"There's the main house, of course, and a barn and bunkhouse and hay shed. Hold on a minute. What else?" he asked Lisl.

"Oh, some smaller buildings with machinery, I think. Not much else. Well, there's the pool with the little house for the filter and stuff. Octavia and Esteban's house. Another garage besides the one with the house. That's where Jerome's truck was. I think that's all."

Brant relayed the information to Hardin.

"Okay, I'll make the warrant as broad as I think the judge will sign off on. And I'll get a warrant for this Jerome's arrest. What's his last name?"

Brant turned to Lisl again. "What's Jerome's last name?"

"I don't know. Jerome is all Colman said when he introduced me."

"Sorry, we don't know. How long do you think it will take to get the warrant?"

"I'd like it to be right now – maybe catch him before he bails out, but realistically it'll probably take awhile, might even be tomorrow. We're going to have to round up quite a crew for this job."

"Be sure to take the cast man – Jim Jerrold's his name, isn't it? You'll want to check out that horse and the truck tires. And to answer your question – yes, I'd like to go along. Let me know when."

"You're at Lisl's?"

"Yes, but I'm going back to my house. I need to get some fresh clothes. These are pretty ratty."

"Don't be dismayed when you get there. I have some people out checking the area and your house. Lisl gave me a key last night, in case you weren't aware of it. Keep me posted if you move somewhere else."

Lisl listened to this exchange and voiced her opposition to the whole idea.

"Brant, you're not thinking of going somewhere with Hardin, are you? He should know better than to ask. You're not well enough to go anywhere. Sometimes I think you men are not too bright."

"You're probably right, but I'd like to go with him. I'll just be riding along in the car – nothing strenuous."

"Oh sure. I've heard that line before. Look at you. Broken bones and shot in the head. I could make a very pertinent remark about people with holes in their head."

Brant reached for her hand and drew her to him.

"You're wonderful to care what happens to a beat-up old cop." He kissed her gently. "Take me home, and let me get cleaned up. You need to go to work anyway. Hardin has to get a search warrant signed so it won't be until later today or maybe not until tomorrow even."

"I can believe Jerome is capable of what you're saying, but I still can't think Colman is mixed up in it. He seems so nice."

"Maybe he's not mixed up in it. Maybe he just has a bad egg for a foreman."

He worked his way up out of the chair and headed for the garage.

"Wait a minute," Lisl objected. "How do we know it's safe for you to go home? What if that man is still around waiting for you?"

"He'd be dumber than I think he is. In the daytime there are too many people around to see him. There are some cops there right now so you know I'll be safe. I'll keep away from the windows if it'll make you feel better. Most of the time I'll be in the bathroom and bedroom trying to get myself presentable to go out in public."

Brant had finished getting himself shaved and clean and was looking for clothes to put on when the phone rang. Probably Hardin. He answered and felt his insides turn over again. The same odd high voice.

"Better get out of town while you still can, or your pretty girl friend is next," and the line went dead.

Rage and fear mixed in his stomach and sent chills up his spine. Brant called Lisl at her office.

"Jerome just called me again and threatened you. Until we catch him, neither of us is safe. I want you to go home and pack a few things and go stay with Westons or Michaels. Or Campbells. We may have to move from one to the other. Call one of them and ask them to come home with you. I don't want you there alone even for a few minutes. And watch to see that you're not followed. I'll let Security know about the threat, and when you know where you'll be, which house, let the cops know."

"Oh, Brant, I can't believe this is happening. That 'I'm really in danger too.' Lisl's voice trembled. "I'll do what you say, but where will you be?"

"If I go out with Hardin today, I'll let you know. If we get that search warrant going, we may catch the beast and it'll all be over. Until then, I'll be here at least for now. The cops are still poking around. They cut the bullet and the wood around it out of the kitchen woodwork. If they leave, I'll go with them somewhere. Take care," Brant grew hoarse, "and I love you."

He pulled on some clothes and went to talk to one of the local Security officers who was helping the deputies. The man assured Brant they would keep a close watch on whichever house Lisl was in and would be suspicious of small dark cars.

Brant then called Hardin to report the latest threat.

"Damn this character. I'm making progress on the search warrant and should have it in hand ready to roll with my whole crew by early afternoon. See you later."

By the time the sheriff's car pulled into his driveway, Brant had eaten a quick sandwich and was ready to go. With a bandage on the side of his head, dark circles under his eyes and a scab on his nose he looked as if he'd been caught in a gang war. He walked carefully and tended to support his left arm across his waist. His usual easy stride had become stiff. I probably look like I'm ninety years old, he thought ruefully.

Chuck Harrison waited for him in the car. Brant was glad it was someone he knew who already was familiar with the case.

"Hi, Brant, you look like you're ready for the old folk's home."

"And you could have gone all day without saying that, you turkey. I was just thinking the same thing myself, but it hurts to hear it's true. It's supposed to be another week or so before I'm likely to get much better, but just you wait. I'll beat you on the golf course again."

At the Justice Center Brant found Hardin and Tony Marcus waiting. They slid in the back seat, and Chuck drove out heading west. Two other police cars plus a pick-up pulled in behind them.

"I brought Tony because he speaks Spanish and because he's been working on this thing as much as we have," Hardin said.

In less than half an hour they turned off the highway to follow the road up to Colman's ranch. Chuck stopped at the gate.

"What now?" he asked.

"Just push that button, and I'll talk to him," Brant answered.

Chuck pushed the button. In a few moments a Spanish-accented voice answered.

"Esteban, this is Brant Grayson. I met you last week when we had dinner with Mr. Lewis. I'd like to see him now."

"Senor Lewis is not here."

"Then I'd like to talk to Jerome."

"He is not here also."

"Then I'll talk with you."

"I cannot open the gate. Jerome tells me not to open for anyone."

"Esteban, I have the police with me. We have a paper from a judge which says you must open the gate and let us in."

"I cannot open."

Brant turned to Tony. "Do you think you can make him understand?"

"I'll try," and he rattled off the Spanish to explain to Esteban why he must follow these orders. After a couple of exchanges, the gate finally slid open, and the police cars drove through and on up the hill.

As they came in sight of the house, Brant felt impressed again with the beauty of the ranch. Tony whistled in appreciation.

"The old owners of the Western Bar S would never recognize the place," Hardin said. "It's an awesome location, and Lewis has done a terrific job remodeling."

Esteban came to the door to meet them. Hardin handed him the search warrant, but he looked at it in comfusion. Tony explained what it was, but Esteban only shook his head.

"I think we want to see the bunkhouse and stable area first," Brant suggested. "Who is here now?" he asked Esteban.

"Only two men and Octavia and me."

"Isn't there a ranch manager?"

"Si, he is not here also."

"Looks like all the pigeons have flown the coop," Hardin said. "Well, let's get at it anyway. Show us where."

"We can drive around," and Brant pointed the way.

CHAPTER TWENTY-ONE

Search Warrant

Two Mexican workmen looked apprehensively from the doorway of the bunkhouse.

"They're probably afraid we're from immigration," Brant said. He turned to Tony. "See if you can reassure them. I couldn't care less right now if they're illegals or not. We just want them not to be afraid to talk to us."

Hardin directed the rest of his crew toward the various buildings to begin their search for whatever might be helpful. The Mexicans stood aside as two of the policemen went into the bunkhouse. Tony motioned for the workmen to sit down with him at the table in the main room. He began to question them, and Brant could see them gradually relax.

Jim Jerrold came from the barn to tell Hardin he was having trouble with the big horse.

"You better get a farrier out here. That elephant of a horse doesn't want to cooperate giving me footprints. I'll go do the truck tires for now."

"Let's go to the house," Hardin said to Brant after he'd called for a farrier. "We should tell that butler – what's his name – to leave the gate open for any other cars we have coming. And we can look around inside – see if we can find anything interesting.

"I think this door must lead into the kitchen area," Brant said. "Let's try it."

Octavia turned in surprise when the two men came into her kitchen. Brant greeted her and introduced Hardin, but she replied with a surly "Buenas tardes". Esteban came in, and Brant told him they wanted to look through the entire house and then would like to see the office.

He led them from the kitchen area into the front hall and from there to the living room.

Hardin whistled softly as he took in the elegant room and the breath-taking view.

"Pretty impressive, isn't it?" Brant said.

"If you tried, you couldn't find a thing to change. It's about as close to perfect as anything could get."

"Here's the elk head," Brant said, and Hardin dragged his gaze away from the view outside the windows.

"I see what you mean. That's some trophy. We'll have to look into who does the taxidermy work."

Brant pointed out the various *objets d'art* in the room.

"I think most of them are perfectly legal, some probably antique. The only one I'd question is this chess set. I'm not sure about the ivory. Obviously it's a contemporary design."

"That'll be an item for the forensic lab. They can tell what kind and age of ivory it is."

The two men checked the dining room. A bouquet of fresh flowers graced the table even though the master of the house wasn't in residence. Hardin looked in the drawers of the buffet but found nothing to catch his eye.

Esteban led them upstairs to the bedrooms. The two guest rooms were invitingly decorated with hand-woven fabrics in desert colors. The closets and bureau drawers were empty. Nothing in the rooms or adjoining bathrooms interested the law.

Colman's own room was about what Brant imagined – masculine but not overwhelmingly so. The windows enjoyed the same stunning view as the living room. The closet and drawers contained just what anyone would expect, clothes suitable for the ranch and a few things for a casual social life. There were a couple of pieces of luggage – empty. A black bearskin rug lay beside the bed to warm Colman's feet.

"I wonder if that bearskin might by chance have come from the bear you found killed," Brant suggested.

"Possible. I'll see if Tony wants to take it along."

The adjoining den was more interesting. A small computer sat on a desk, a comfortable chair alongside plus some book shelves. Interspersed among the books were various foreign objects. Brant couldn't bring himself to put them under the heading of "knick-knacks". They were much too lovely and probably expensive. It occurred to him that maybe if you had Colman's income and life style, this is what your knick-knacks look like.

"Some of these should be examined," he said. "This little framed picture for instance." Brilliantly colored feathers made an intricate design within the frame. "Feathers from exotic bird species mostly aren't legal."

"And this tortoise shell letter opener," Hardin said as he looked over the desk. The drawers contained nothing out of the ordinary. "We'll take these things along," and he picked up the feather picture and letter opener.

"Might be something interesting on the computer," Brant speculated.

"Let's see the office first," Hardin said. "I'll call and get one of our computer whiz kids out here."

The two men followed Esteban back downstairs and down a short hallway behind the kitchen into a modest size room filled with a desk, file cabinets, computer, fax and assorted other business machines.

"The manager," Brant asked Esteban, "where is he?"

"Senor Wilson will return soon. He is gone only to town for supplies."

"Thank you. Please leave the gate open since we are expecting another car. We'll want to talk to the manager when he gets here."

"Si," Esteban nodded and remained in the doorway watching.

Hardin went to the file cabinets and began to look through them methodically. Brant sat in the desk chair to rest while he studied the room.

"I'm not even sure just what I'm looking for," Hardin said after a few minutes. "Something that might tell us if Lewis is running Jerome's show or if he's an innocent bystander."

"When the manager gets here, we may find a few answers."

Tony came to the door. "Here you are. I've been looking for you. A body could get lost in this place. I've found out a few things from the Mexicans, Carlos and Manuel. Once I convinced them we weren't planning to send them back to Mexico, they've been very helpful."

"Do you think they're part of the hunting operation?"

"Nah, they're strictly hired help, but they know a considerable amount about the ranch. Jerome left this morning. He packed some gear in the car. It's a small, black Toyota probably about five years old. There's a dirt track that leads out to the highway beyond the fields. Mostly used for farm machinery. It's fenced along the highway so that you wouldn't know a car could get through just looking at it casually. He went out that way, and for all we know, he could be into California by now."

"I don't suppose they knew the car license number."

"No such luck," Tony answered. "They don't even know his last name. And they said that sometimes he would drive off in his dualy and be gone four or five days. The guys searching the bunkhouse haven't come up with anything helpful either. His room is reasonably neat. There are clothes left behind but no rifles or ammunition. Carlos said Jerome took a sleeping bag and two rifles with him. They didn't see any other camping gear. There's no desk or anything like that in his room. No letters or bills. No personal files like tax stuff."

"He must have records, bank books, things like that somewhere," Hardin said. "I think we better get a search warrant for that house of Jack Jones' in town. No reason now not to. Maybe he stores things there. Now that I think of it, maybe that's where he is. I'll get Chuck on it."

"Maybe," Brant ventured, "what we're looking for is all in this room. Maybe the ranch manager keeps the records for the whole staff. It wouldn't hurt to go through that house, but I can't imagine he'd hole up there right in the middle of town."

"Manuel and Carlos have shown the guys searching the barn which saddles belong to which horses," Tony told them. "I asked which horses participated in the hunts last fall. They weren't sure about all four of them, but they pointed out three. We've loaded those saddles and blankets in the pick-up. There'll be blood we can find in the stitching to match up at the lab. Now the boys are looking over the horse trailer. Along with the dualy."

The sound of a car in the driveway interrupted them and then voices in the kitchen. An angry young man came into the office.

"Just exactly what is going on here? What are you doing in my office going through my files? And what are all those policemen doing prowling around the buildings?"

"I'm Lt. Hardin Metcalf, deputy sheriff for Les Rapides County. This is Sr. Trooper Tony Marcus from the Oregon State Police and Brant Grayson, a friend of Mr. Lewis. He's helping us with our inquiry. We have a duly authorized search warrant for these premises. We gave it to the butler when we arrived. He gave it back to us, and here it is for your information. Are you the manager?"

"Yes," he answered absently as he read through the warrant. "I'm Nicholas Wilson. Well, this seems to be in order. I'm not sure what help I can give you or what the hell you think you're looking for."

"A couple of questions first. We're interested in finding your ranch foreman, Jerome. Can you tell us his last name?"

"Sure, it's Billings. What d'you need him for? Where's he gone? I haven't seen him since first thing this morning."

"He's wanted on suspicion of murder."

"Murder! I always thought Jerome was kind of mean, but not that mean. Who'd he supposedly kill?"

Hardin ignored that question to ask another of his own. "Mr. Lewis, do you know where he is?"

"Yes, today he's in Singapore, tomorrow in Bangkok, then Hong Kong and home. Should be in San Francisco by the weekend and maybe here next week."

"Can you get word to him? I think it would be advisable if he returned here immediately."

"Let's see, it's Wednesday morning over there now. Maybe I can catch him before he goes out for the day. He isn't gonna like what's going on here, y'know. And he isn't gonna like coming home in the middle of a buying trip."

Nicholas flipped through a small phone file, found the number he wanted and punched it in on the desk phone.

"Good morning. Please connect me with Mr. Colman Lewis." Nicholas drummed his fingers on the desk as he waited for the connection. "Colman, good morning, this is Nicholas. Sorry to call so early, but something has come up here. There are policemen all over the place. They have a search warrant, and they're looking for Jerome. They think he's killed someone. I told them your schedule, but they seem to think it would be a good idea if you'd come home right away – skip the other cities."

Brant could hear Colman's voice but not the words.

"Yes, I know," Nicholas said, "I told them you wouldn't be happy about this." He listened. "No, Jerome isn't here. I haven't seen him since early this morning."

The words might not have been distinct from the other end of the phone line, but there was no mistaking the outraged sound of Colman's voice.

Nicholas asked, "Do you want to talk to one of the policemen?"

"Here," and he handed the phone to Hardin.

"Good morning, Mr. Lewis. This is Lt. Hardin Metcalf of the Les Rapides County Sheriff's Office. We have good reason to suspect that your foreman, Jerome Billings, has killed two men and also that he has participated in illegal killings of elk. With our search warrant we are looking for further evidence. It would be advisable for you to return here as soon as possible."

Hardin listened to Colman who, Brant surmised, must have asked why this concerned him so urgently.

"Because, sir, the man is in your employ, and some of the evidence may implicate you."

"Here," and he handed the phone back to Nicholas, "he wants to talk to you again."

As Nicholas finished the conversation, Hardin turned to Brant and Tony. "That last bit about him possibly being implicated got his attention. He'll see what he can do about a flight back."

Nicholas put the phone down and turned to the men. "He'll try to arrange about changing his flights. He'll be coming into San Francisco and will call you when he gets here."

"How does he get here from the airport?" Hardin asked. "Does he have a car there, or does someone have to pick him up?"

"He leaves a car there. What more do you need to know?"

"You can help us with information about how the ranch runs. In searching Jerome's quarters, we have found no personal records like wage statements, tax records, no personal correspondence, bills, bank statements. He must have that sort of thing somewhere."

"I keep all the business records in the computer and do the tax and social security filing for all the help. I can't tell you where he might keep any bank statements. I'm sure he has a bank account somewhere. He's paid by check each month. As to any personal correspondence, I'm not surprised you haven't found any. I don't think you will. He has no next-of-kin listed with me and doesn't seem to have any friends. He gets an occasional phone call, I think, but I can't tell you who from."

"What other records do you keep in this computer? Only about the ranch, or about other parts of Mr. Lewis' business affairs?"

"This is strictly ranch records. His business records are all handled in San Francisco.

"Okay, so much for that for now. We're also

interested in the illegal killing of elk and the possible sale of trophy heads. What can you tell us about that?"

"What makes you think I can tell you anything about something like that?" Nicholas asked.

"Our evidence indicates some of the elk meat which came from an illegal kill has been served in this house. Also Mr. Lewis has a mounted head which he said he shot but for which he did not have a legal tag."

"Saying he shot that elk was just a little bragging. It came from Jerome, and so did the meat. If it all wasn't legal, he's the one to blame, not Colman."

"Where was the taxidermy work done?" Hardin asked.

"I have no idea. Jerome took care of all that, and I paid him cash which was the way he wanted it. He wanted enough to pay the guy who helped him with the hunt, too."

"Was this the first time for a transaction like that?"

"No, he's done it before, and Colman always told me to just pay him what he asked." Nicholas shrugged. "I don't know what the money went for – helpers, taxidermy, whatever. I didn't think it was a very good way to handle business – just shelling out cash like that, but Colman seemed to think it was okay. Just for my own information I entered the amounts in the computer."

"That could be helpful," Tony said. Brant sat quietly listening to the exchange.

"I think Jerome was selling the trophy heads somewhere at a big mark-up," Nicholas continued. "I don't know who he sold them to or for how much or where all the profit - if any - went. If he repaid Colman for what I gave him, it didn't come through here, or at least not so I recognized it. It might have been lumped in with some other entry, or perhaps it went into the accounts in San Francisco."

"Does this ranch operate at a profit?"

"Hell no. Does your home operate at a profit? It's the same thing. This is Colman's home, and he runs it for pleasure. He has a condo in San Fran, but this is where he really likes to be. He invested a bundle in the house and all the other buildings. The horses sometimes make money, and occasionally he sells a llama or two. The alfalfa and hay go to feed the stock. No, this isn't a money-making proposition. The funds come from the export-import stuff."

Hardin shook his head. "Must be nice to have a business lucrative enough to pay for all this."

"Do you know," Brant asked, "where the chess set in the living room came from?"

"The Orient somewhere. I think it was a gift from someone Colman trades with over there. Neat, isn't it?"

"Since trade in new ivory isn't legal, we will have to take it with us to be tested," Hardin said. "Also there are other items we're taking. We will give you an inventory of all that we take."

"Well, hey now, when do we get stuff back that you're taking? Can you just walk off with anything you see?"

"Only things that, in our estimation, are evidence in this case. If, after we've examined objects, we find they aren't related, they'll be returned immediately. Anything that turns out to be evidence will be kept until the case is settled, including any appeals."

"You're talking months and years there," Nicholas objected. "What kinds of things are you talking about?"

"Anything that appears to be made of animal parts that are illegal to kill, and the vehicles, saddles, etc. that were likely used in the elk hunts as well as the mounted head in the living room."

"Do you by chance still have any elk meat in the freezer?" Brant asked.

"I don't know," Nicholas said. "How about it, Esteban? Any elk meat left?"

"Si, senor."

"We'll want that too," Hardin told him.

The noise of large engines came to them from the stable courtyard. Nicholas jumped up to look out the window. A tow truck was getting hitched to the horse trailer. In it were the saddles and horse blankets.

"You're taking the trailer? And saddles? What in hell for?"

"We'll be looking to see if the blood on them matches the elk meat you have here and the samples we have from the illegal kills."

"You won't find any blood on the saddles or the trailer. Jerome always had the Mexicans clean everything up well after he'd used them."

"It's impossible to clean them well enough that traces won't be found," Hardin assured him.

As Nicholas watched out the window, the first tow truck moved off down the driveway with the horse trailer, and another moved up to take Jerome's dual-wheel pick-up truck including the canopy top.

He moved away from the window shaking his head in disbelief. "You guys don't do things halfway, do you? Colman won't be happy about losing the horse trailer, and if Jerome shows up again, he'll be livid about that truck. It's his pride and joy."

Nicholas scratched his head. "And you tell me – what are we supposed to do without the trailer if we have to move some horses in or out? I'll have to think of something – maybe rent one for awhile. Damn! I wonder if insurance covers this sort of thing." He sat down at his desk. "I always thought this job was pretty peaceful and non-stressful, but you've managed to change that in a hurry."

"Sorry if we're making life harder for you," Hardin apologized. Brant smiled slightly. He noted a certain lack of sincerity in Hardin's apology.

"We'll need a ladder to remove that elk head in the living room. I assume there is one somewhere."

"Sure, in one of the tool sheds. Esteban, go help the policemen get that elk head off the wall, and bring the frozen elk meat too. Now, anything else?" Nicholas sounded like his patience was wearing thin.

"We are bringing one of our computer specialists to look at your files as well as the one upstairs."

"I can show him anything he's interested in here. As for the one in Colman's den, it's personal, and I've never used it."

"Thank you for your cooperation. We'll get that inventory finished up and get a copy to you in a little while," Hardin said as he rose to go back outside. Brant and Tony followed him. At the door Brant turned back with a last question for Nicholas.

"Incidentally, is Jerome left-handed?"

"Well, yes, he is. How'd you know to ask?"

"Just wondered," Brant Answered and went on out. When they were out of earshot, Hardin smiled. "That's another little detail confirmed against him. What do you guys think about that manager and the rest of the staff?"

"Everybody's being about as helpful as you could expect," Tony said. "The cook looks kinda sour, but otherwise, no problem. I think we have everything we need out of here for evidence."

"What about you, Brant? You think that manager's as straightforward as he sounds?" Hardin asked.

"So far. I'll be interested in how much cash he's paid Jerome for elk heads. If this was very often, there must be a market for them beyond this area. Sounds fishy to me that Colman was willing to pay him in cash. I don't know much about the taxidermy business. I suppose there are some who aren't averse to making extra money outside the regulations. How about it, Tony?"

"Sure, like any other business. Some are honest all day, and some are shady. Any hunter with a legal trophy would expect to pay up front for getting it mounted, but if it wasn't legal, maybe he sells it to the taxidermist who then mounts it and sells it at a profit to anyone who wants it or to someone like Jerome who knows where he can get big money exporting it out of the area or maybe overseas."

"That might explain why Colman is willing to pay him cash," Brant said. "The whole transaction would need to be cash. Of course, shipping an elk head wouldn't be easy. You can't exactly hide it in a bunch of toys or machinery parts. Well, on the other hand, maybe you could with the right facilities, and it's possible that might be what Jerome was doing when he was gone for a few days now and then. Taking some trophies somewhere to sell. It's not going to be easy to nail down."

Another car pulled up, and a young man stepped out. Hardin introduced him as Ralph Cober, the computer specialist.

"The machine in the office shouldn't be a problem," Hardin told him. "The manager is willing to take you through it, but you better keep your eye out for any signs of his hiding something. We want a rundown on the finances of the place as well as anything that might pertain to the owner's business in San Francisco. Especially we want anything about Jerome Billings, the foreman we think has killed two men already. There's another computer in the upstairs den, and you're on your own with that one. Tinker away and see if you can get into it. We'll be finishing up here soon, but take as long as you need."

Hardin told Ralph where to find the office and then headed for the bunkhouse. He sat down at the table to make his inventory with the help of all the officers. Brant eased himself down. It had been a long day, and he felt worn out. Worried too. He looked around for a telephone. One hung on the wall in the kitchen end of the room. With an effort he pushed himself up again and went to call the security office in Rivermount.

"Brant Grayson, Chief. How are things in Rivermount? All quiet, I hope."

"No sign of your shooter. Didn't really expect any during the day. Are you coming back tonight?"

"Soon, I hope. We're nearly finished here. The perp's name is Jerome Billings, but he's taken off. Left this morning. No idea where. We have a bulletin out for him statewide and in California and Washington. Anyway, where is Lisl staying?"

"She's at Weston's and they're expecting you too."

"That's great. Tell them I should be there in two hours or less, and thanks for all you help."

CHAPTER TWENTY-TWO

Wednesday

The evening at Weston's passed uneventfully.
Brant felt too tired to give them more than a cursory rundown of the day. He didn't want to bring Colman into it
yet in case it turned out he had no criminal intent.

He ate a late supper they had saved for him and
went to bed as quickly as he could. Caro had put Lisl and
Brant in separate bedrooms. He wondered if it was her
inate sense of propriety, or if she didn't know they had
been sleeping together occasionally. Actually he was glad
she'd arranged things that way. He ached too much and
was too tired to be good company for anyone.

Next day they were scheduled to move to Michaels'
house. Brant thought it probably wasn't necessary to keep
up this charade. He felt sure Jerome had put as much
distance as possible between himself and the Farwell area
by now. On the other hand, maybe he had holed up
somewhere not too far away. With the bulletins out about
him all up and down the West Coast, he would run a
definite risk of someone recognizing him when he stopped
for gas. Maybe that would happen soon, Brant hoped, and
they could resume a normal life.

Wednesday morning took a leisurely turn, and the
whole day stretched ahead with nothing pressing – a good
time to rest body and mind.

Lisl left for work around nine o'clock with a member of Rivermount's security force following her. No one expected Jerome to take a shot at her from somewhere along the way. Too many residents and tourists would be roaming around, but it did no harm to let him know – just in case he was watching – that it wasn't going to be easy to carry out his threat against her.

Brant and Jud read the morning newspaper along with their second cups of coffee while Caro bustled around in the kitchen and bedrooms. Brant appreciated the time to relax. He noticed a gradual improvement with his injuries. The sickly green color had nearly faded out around his eyes, and the bruise on his forehead was hidden by his hair. His ribs still kept him from taking a deep breath or moving abruptly, but the constant pain he had felt right after the accident had eased. The broken collarbone still bothered him. Having only one arm that functioned properly was a nuisance. The only good thing was that at least the bad arm wasn't his right arm.

Jud and Brant chatted about news in the paper, sports results, weather prospects, and Brant took time to arrange for the repair of the window and kitchen woodwork at his house. He swiveled his chair around to look when Jud noticed half a dozen deer parading across the golf course.

"Caro isn't going to be happy if they eat up her flowers," Jud said. The deer were both a constant delight and aggravation to the Rivermount residents.

Brant read some more, but then his eyes drifted shut. His mind sorted through all they'd learned yesterday. Even without the rifles for ballistic comparison, all evidence pointed to Jerome as the murderer of both Jake and Barney as well as an unknown number of elk. And he came within an inch of murdering Brant too. Where would he be likely to have gone? If he was smart, he'd put as many miles as possible between himself and Central Oregon. If he drove hard enough, he could even be in Mexico by now. Or he could have left the car in the Bay Area and flown to Mexico. He was certainly smart enough not to drive his white dualy which was much too memorable and easily spotted. But if he had stopped for gas anywhere or bought a plane ticket, the police might have picked up his trail.

Then again what about the sleeping bag? Did he know of some place to camp? Heaven knows there are endless places in the vast tracts of forest spreading in all directions. Just a sleeping bag wouldn't be enough for camping out. Did he know of a cabin somewhere? Brant wasn't familiar enough with the area yet, but he knew there were cabins scattered around Indian Lake where they'd skied last winter. Probably there were plenty of others on private property as well as national and state forest land. Tony or Hardin would know, he thought as he dozed off.

Caro gently wakened him.

"It's time for you to move on," she giggled. "Not that we wouldn't love to have you stay longer, but Michaels are expecting you, and we're ready to go. Jud has Lisl's things in the car."

"Oh sure, guess I must have dozed off. I'll get my gear ready."

When they were in the car, Brant asked if they could go by his house to pick up a few more clothes. As he opened the door, he could hear the phone ringing. Probably Hardin.

He picked up the phone, but no one answered his hello. He could hear the sound of someone breathing plus vague noises in the background. His heart beat hard as fear crawled along the back of his neck, but he tried to place the sounds he could hear. Voices, maybe, and traffic noise before the line went dead. He slumped against the desk as he put his phone down.

"Brant, what is it?" Caro asked frantically. "You look terrible. Was it another one of those calls?"

Brant nodded.

"Oh, Jud, what can we do? What did the call say?"

"Nothing, this time. He didn't say anything. How did he know where to find me? Someone must be following us." His heart still pounded, and for a moment he felt almost as frantic as Caro looked.

"I'll get the clothes I want, and then let's get out of here."

When they were back in the car, Brant tried to watch behind them, but no one seemed to be following. Jud headed for the post office.

Brant picked up his mail and Lisl's. As he came out he looked across the parking lot, and his heart took another jolt. It wasn't Jerome this time. It was Frank parked on the far side. There was no reason why he shouldn't be there. The post office and shopping mall were open to the public. On the other hand, why should he be there? He lived and worked in Lakeside fifteen miles south, and Rivermount had little to draw him here.

In a flash Brant realized what was going on. Jerome was out of touch, but he'd delegated Frank to keep up the pressure. Damn the man!

They were no sooner inside the door at Michaels before Caro told them of the latest call.

"Angie and Doc, it's so awful. That person is still after Brant. He just called again. I can't believe this is happening to all of us. Oh, Jud, I'm scared now too. I didn't think he knew us, but maybe he does."

Brant tried to reassure her. "I think I know what's going on at least right now. He doesn't know your names, any of you. He's using a phone in his car. And it isn't the same man. I don't think you have to worry, but I'd like to phone Hardin."

Doc showed him to a phone in the den. Hardin wasn't in, but the dispatcher said she would get a message to him and for Brant to wait by the phone. In a few minutes it rang.

"What now?" Hardin asked.

"Another call." Brant could hear Hardin's growl. "But it wasn't Jerome this time. I'm sure it was Frank, and he's using a phone in his car while following me around," and Brant told him how it had happened.

"Did Frank know you saw him?"

"I'm not sure."

"Doesn't matter. We'll go lean on him again. I'll tighten the screws a little and see if we can scare something out of him. He must know where Jerome is."

"Anything else new?" Brant asked. "Did Ralph get some good stuff out of the computers?"

"Yes, but we haven't had time to analyze it yet. I have people out checking at all the banks in the area to see if we can find Jerome's account. Tony took all the stuff – the saddles and elk meat, blood samples from the dualy and horse trailer, the elk head, the other imported things we took from the house – to Ashland this morning. He's going to stay there until he gets the results. There isn't much else we can do until Lewis gets here."

"No," Brant agreed. "At the very best he couldn't make it here before tonight, more likely sometime tomorrow."

"You're at Michaels now? I'll keep you posted if we find out anything from Frank or from the bank search."

The rest of the day proved non-traumatic. No more threatening phone calls. No gun shots in the night. Just pleasant company with good friends. Lisl had a convention in town and didn't come home for lunch but managed to leave in time for dinner. Doc had changed the dressing on Brant's head and pronounced that the wound was healing nicely. The men played gin rummy for awhile, and Brant put the criminal world out of his mind at the cost of losing $1.35 to Doc.

During their happy hour before dinner Lisl heard the latest on the phone call to Brant. He reassured them that he knew who this one was from, and the police had it well in hand. Lisl even acted like she believed him this time and didn't think he was just trying to allay her fears.

After the restful afternoon Brant could almost feel his bones growing back together. The events of the past week nagged at the back of his mind, but for now he felt relaxed and happy. Especially since he'd noticed Angie had put Lisl in the same bedroom with him. Either her perception was greater than Caro's or her sense of propriety was less.

Friday

Hardin called Brant Thursday morning with the latest reports.

"We sat hard on Frank but didn't get much. He insists he doesn't know where Jerome is, barely knows the man. Says he's been in the tavern only once or twice. He admits being in Rivermount yesterday but says he was there to shop. Not very likely but hard to refute. He has a cellular phone but denies he called you. We'll check on that, and we'll get him on something yet, but so far we haven't made a dent."

"A hard nut to crack," Brant said.

"Sure is. I don't think you have to worry about him making more phone calls to you though. He won't risk it now that he knows we're onto that little scheme. While we were talking to him, I sent some of the other guys out to see if any of the regulars at the bar knew Billings. Most of them said they had seen him a couple of times maybe. They knew him as Jack Jones but recognized our description. Nobody seemed to know anything about him. Some wanted to know if we'd found who killed Barney. One suggested it was probably that Grady Brown fella who hadn't been around for awhile."

"I thought they'd figure that. Do you have anything on the bank account and the computer stuff?"

"Now that has been a little more productive than our visit with Frank. Billing's account is at one of the banks in the town next south of Lakeside. They helpfully provided us with a rundown of the action on the account for the past couple of years. Aside from his paycheck there are deposits which correspond roughly with the payouts of cash that Nicholas made to him. What he deposited each time was less than Nicholas gave him of course, since he had to pay Barney and the taxidermist, but it added up to a tidy amount over the months. There were some in the summer which were probably for antlers in velvet, and there wouldn't have been any taxidermy for those. When we ever find the guy, we have enough evidence to convict him two or three ways. But none of it tells us yet if Lewis is in on it too."

"And you haven't heard from him yet?"

"No, I called that manager this morning. He says Lewis was on a flight that would get him into San Fran this morning but that he had some things he had to tend to there today and won't get the commuter up here until late tonight. He'll call us in the morning. I guess that's the best we can do."

"Okay, then I'll see you tomorrow."

"Sure thing. As soon as I hear from him, I'll send Chuck out for you, and we'll have a go at the guy. See ya."

Brant and Lisl moved on over to Campbell's house. Brant felt sure there wasn't anything to fear anymore, but as long as it was arranged, he figured they might as well go on as planned.

On the way over, he asked Doc to stop by his own house. He wanted to be there for awhile just to see if the phone would ring again. After half an hour he was ready to leave. Frank wasn't following him around with his cellular phone today. Doc had his hand on the door when the ringing started. It could be anybody, Brant thought as he headed for the kitchen desk.

"Don't think I've forgotten you." The same high voice but sounding faint and far away.

"Damn you!" Brant yelled.

The voice laughed, a high sinister giggle, before the line went dead. Brant ran his hand up his face and through his hair forgetting about the bruise on his forehead. It hurt, and he winced. His eyes as he turned back to Doc had gone to steel-gray points of hate.

"Him again?" Doc asked.

"Doc, that man is turning me into something I don't want to be. I hate him, and I don't like that. In all my years with the police department I can't remember feeling personal, deep hatred like this for another human being. Right now I'm not the kind of person I want to be," and he turned away to gaze out the window. Golfers going by in the sunshine on the fairway seemed a world away.

Doc came to stand by him. After a couple of minutes he put his hand on Brant's shoulder.

"Come on, let's go to Campbells. It's okay for you to feel that way now. It won't change you. Hate him because he's a hateful person. You'll be back to your real person when you catch him. This is temporary."

"What if we never catch him? Some cases are like that. The guilty one is never found." He'd worked on a few that were still unsolved on the books when he'd retired. Brant didn't want to think this could be one of those.

"You'll get him," Doc reassured him and led him out to the car.

The minute they were in the door at Campbell's, Brant asked to use the phone. He had to let Hardin know there'd been another call.

"Hardin, I had another call from Jerome. He said he hadn't forgotten me."

"You're kidding! Where was he calling from? Could you tell?"

"Not for sure. He sounded kind of far away like maybe a bad connection. Do you suppose he might have a cellular phone and be calling from where he might be camping out in the woods?"

"Sounds possible. Could he have been calling long distance, though? Maybe he's all the way to Mexico and just wants to keep you scared. He's mean enough."

"That could be too, I suppose." Brant sighed. "Well, I just wanted to let you know. It's not much help. Maybe Lewis will have an idea. Call if you hear anything."

The normalcy of Campbell's home gave Brant a sense of calm. His taut nerves relaxed slowly. Amber waved her tail joyfully, delighted to see him.

Elaine planned for him to share the bedroom with Lisl, and he felt suddenly, overwhelmingly grateful. He needed her soft warm body beside him, the fresh smell of her hair, her smooth skin to touch and her lips to kiss. She would wash away all the vicious hate, make it disappear in the night. Until then he would put it all out of his mind.

It was nearly ten o'clock Friday morning before Hardin called.

"Lewis phoned a few minutes ago. Wants us to come to his house. You ready?"

"Yes, but you don't need to send Chuck out. Phil and Elaine are coming to town anyway this morning, and they'll drop me off."

"Let's go," Hardin said when Brant came into the office. "I want to meet this guy. Tony's coming too. On the way out he can tell you the results of his visit to the U. S. Forensic lab."

When they were settled in Hardin's car and out on the road, Brant couldn't be patient any longer.

"What did you find out, Tony?"

"Plenty. The elk meat matches, as we suspected it would. The head matches the cut edges on one of the hides from the kill you found. The ivory is elephant and new, not antique. The letter opener isn't tortoise, it's turtle from one of the endangered species, and the feathers are mostly from a variety of parrots and some other tropical birds, all protected species. Oh, yes, and the bear skin is from that kill we found with the bullets that matched the others. That covers everything, I think, and makes the whole ball game illegal."

"What about the saddles?" Brant wanted to know.

"Oh yeah, forgot that part. All the blood samples from the saddles, the trailer and the dualy came from one or another of the kills we found. We've got that guy coming and going if we can just lay our hands on him."

The ranch gate opened for them, and Esteban waited at the front door to greet them.

"Senor Lewis is expecting you," he told them.

Colman came through the front hall from the back of the house. "Brant, nice to see you again," he said as he held out his hand.

Brant introduced Hardin and Tony, and Colman led them into the living room. He wore khaki pants and a denim work shirt, but Brant marveled that somehow Colman managed to make the work clothes look well-groomed. Octavia must take good care of his wardrobe as well as the kitchen.

Colman directed them to a semi-circle of chairs facing the windows and the spectacular view. Before they were well seated Esteban appeared bearing a tray with coffee and small cakes. He passed the refreshments and then quietly left the room.

"We're sorry to have to interrupt your business. How was the trip back? Not too much jet lag?" Hardin asked.

"Oh no, I never have any problem with that anymore. I've been crossing time zones so much for so many years that my body has quit objecting," Colman assured them, but Brant thought he looked tired. Dark circles shadowed his eyes.

"Beautiful place you have here," Hardin said, "and your staff seems to take very good care of it in your absence."

"Thank you, I'm glad you like it," their host replied. "I've been fortunate with the staff so far. Esteban and Octavia have been with me for years. The other two Mexicans are relatives of theirs. Nicholas was originally from Portland, and he's been handling the management of the ranch ever since I bought it. But Jerome, now, that's a problem. He's been an excellent foreman. I'm upset finding a difficulty with him. Please tell me what this is all about."

"I'm afraid you are going to be in the market for a new foreman," Hardin said. "We have evidence which indicates he has killed two men, shot at Brant and caused Brant's car to run off a cliff putting Brant in the hospital and totaling his car."

Colman looked shocked. "Brant, I had no idea. Are you all right now? I thought you seemed just a little stiff."

"Some cracked and broken ribs and a broken collarbone. Those will cut into my golf season. This," and he fingered the bandage on his head, "came from the shot he took at me in my house. Otherwise, I'm okay. However, when he shot me, he narrowly missed Lisl. He's also threatened both of us on the phone."

"I'm devastated. Please accept my sincere apology. And he has involved Lisl in this too? It's too terrible to think about. You said something about elk being killed. What's that all about?"

"Along with the murders," Hardin continued, "we have evidence that he has been killing elk illegally. The elk meat you had here in your house is from one of those kills as well as the trophy head you had on the wall."

Colman shook his head, and Brant noticed a weariness in him. His shoulders slumped just a fraction, and the circles under his eyes deepened.

"It's so hard to believe. I don't know much about Jerome's background. An acquaintance in California recommended him. He had been living there but had moved to this area about the time I bought the ranch. He is not a friendly person, very taciturn, keeps to himself. But he knows how to run the ranch. He's familiar with planting and harvesting and with the animals, and he seems to know how to manage the help too. Carlos and Manuel are here most of the time. They go back to visit their families in the winter for awhile. And we hire others when we need them at busy times."

"Were you aware that Jerome liked to hunt?"

"Oh yes, of course. He'd be off now and then in the fall. He kept us supplied with venison and birds as well as elk occasionally. I had no idea he was killing any of it illegally."

"The mounted head you had? Where did it come from?"

"Jerome gave it to me last fall – said he just wanted me to have it since it was such a beauty."

"Brant was under the impression you had killed it."

Colman reddened. "I shouldn't have said that. I guess I just wanted to impress my new friends. I'm really not a hunter at all."

"Where did he get it mounted?"

"I have no idea about that. I never thought to ask."

"And the meat?"

"Same thing. Jerome brought it in late last fall, and we froze part of it."

"Mr. Wilson, your manager, tells us that you authorized him to pay Jerome cash occasionally for trophy heads he had mounted and then sold. Were you aware of what the money was for?"

Colman squirmed around in his chair. "Yes, more or less. He came to me the first fall after I hired him. Asked if he could borrow some money. Said he had a chance to make a good bit and he'd pay it back in a short while. When I asked him what kind of business he was into, he said he bought heads from other hunters, paid to have them mounted and then sold them at a profit."

"Did you ever wonder if this was legal?"

"The first time he asked about borrowing the money to buy the heads, I questioned him about it, and he assured me it was all right. He said the hunters he bought them from all had tags. He wanted the cash because that's what the hunters wanted and the taxidermists too. I assumed they just wanted to keep the money out of their income tax statements."

"Didn't you wonder about payments in the summer?"

"In the summer? Oh no, I didn't realize there's been any then. I'm not a hunter, but even I know hunting season is in the fall. I didn't know about any payments in the summer."

"Did Jerome ever repay these loans you made to him?"

"Yes, but to my San Francisco office."

"Why was that?"

"Well," Colman shifted his position again, "the first time, he gave me the money just as I was leaving here on a trip, and I took it along. After that it just seemed easier to keep on the same way."

Hardin turned to Tony. "Do you want to take over here about the other items?"

"Yes. Mr. Lewis, about the chess set, the letter opener and the feather picture. They were on the inventory of items we removed during our search last Tuesday. You're aware we took them?"

"Yes, Nicholas showed me the list this morning, although I'm mystified about how they relate to all this business about Jerome and the elk."

"How did you happen to have those items? Where did they come from?"

"They were gifts from people I do business with in Asia. All of them are just keepsakes from friends."

"It happens they are all made from birds or animals that are illegal to kill or to trade in. I wonder how you managed to get them into the country without customs people finding them."

"Illegal! I can't believe that. They're things that are readily available in various countries. Anyone could buy similar things, I think. It just happens mine were gifts. I've dealt for years with the people who gave them to me. As for how I got them into the country, I don't know. I guess no one asked me about them, and I had no idea they weren't legal. I find this all very hard to believe and the implications of it very unpleasant. I'm getting the feeling that you think I've personally been involved in some nefarious schemes."

"Your personal involvement will be looked into, Mr. Lewis," Hardin said. "Right now, we'd like to see if you can help us find Jerome."

"Yes, and I can't tell you how sorry I am about Brant being hurt. Are you sure Jerome's the one?"

"I'm sure," Brant answered. "I've seen him more than once. He even had the gall to come to the hospital to threaten me."

Colman looked horrified. "And how is Lisl involved?"

"Simply because she knows me, apparently," Brant answered meeting Colman's eyes. Colman looked away.

"But how did you become involved? I thought you are retired from police work."

"A group of us happened on one of the illegal elk kills. A chain of circumstances."

"Brant has been most cooperative in helping us with this case," Hardin said. "The local law enforcement community is more than willing to accept help from retired police who may have special expertise."

"Well, under the circumstances, I'm only too happy to try to help you find Jerome. I will miss him as a fore-man, but if all your accusations are correct, he certainly should be brought to justice. I'm not sure I can be much help, though. Nicholas says he took off last Tuesday morning before you people got here and hasn't been seen since."

"Do you have any idea where he might have gone? Any family or friends who might take him in?"

"No, not that I can think of. I don't think he has any family at all. He used to take a few days off now and then, but I don't know where he went. Otherwise, except for the days off during hunting season, he was mostly around here."

"We understand he took a sleeping bag with him. Would he be likely to be camping out somewhere?"

"That's possible, I suppose. He's a man who always seemed at home in the wilds. But no, if he were going camping, I think he'd have taken his truck, and Nicholas tells me he drove his little old Toyota."

"Probably he didn't take the truck because it is so readily identifiable, and he knew we'd recognize it."

"Now, let me think." Colman gazed out the window, tapping his finger on his teeth. "Just maybe," he said after a minute, "I'm remembering something. He has – or at least used to have – a little cabin out in the woods. He took me there once when I'd first hired him. Maybe he's there."

Brant could see Hardin and Tony come alive with anticipation.

"Could you tell us where it is?"

"I'm not sure," Colman said hesitantly. "He drove when we went there, and I didn't pay much attention since I was new in the area and didn't know my way around. I know we went through town and on past the turn-off to Rivermount. And then we turned west off the highway before Lakeside. After that I'm vague."

"I have a Forest Service map in the car," Tony said and left to get it. Colman refilled the coffee cups and passed the cakes around again while they waited for Tony to return. When he came back, he spread the map out on the table toward Colman and guided him through the possible area.

"Do you know if his cabin is on state or national forest land or private?"

"I think maybe private. I vaguely remember a sign saying 'Leaving the Les Rapides National Forest' shortly before we came to the cabin."

"Okay," Tony said as he pointed to a line on the map, "this is the Forest Service boundary. Now if you left the highway between Rivermount and Lakeside, did you go on a paved road?"

"For awhile, quite awhile. Then it was a gravel and then just dirt. There was a small creek running along beside the cabin. I think he got his water from it. It's in a clearing, no trees or brush near the house, but lots of trees and undergrowth around. There's another building, a garage maybe or shed not too far from the house. And an outhouse off toward the trees."

"How big a place is the house?" Hardin asked.

"Not big, really just one room. He built it himself and had been living there before he came to live here when I hired him."

"Thank you for your information," Hardin said. "We can take the map back to the office and figure out where you're talking about. We'll be in touch. Plan to stay in the area for now," and the three men made their way to the front door. Esteban held it open for them.

"What d'you think?" Hardin asked when they were on the way back to town. "Is he in it or not?"

"He sure had an answer for everything," Tony said. "I don't know whether to swallow it all whole or not."

"Like Tony says," Brant said, "he seems innocent and sincere and wanting to be helpful, but I find it hard to believe that a businessman would pay out cash like that unless he was very sure what he was paying for. And also it strikes me as odd that a man whose business is exporting and importing isn't more aware of the customs regulations.

Of course, the fact that he has a few artifacts here that were illegal to import still doesn't tie him to Jerome's affairs. Our first priority is to nail Jerome, and then we can turn our attention to Colman's connection, if any."

Rain began to splatter on the windshield as they drove back to Farwell.

CHAPTER TWENTY-FOUR

Friday Evening

"Let's stop at your cop shop," Hardin said to Tony as they neared town. "Your office has more room to spread out the map and see if any of your guys recognize the place."

Rain came down harder as they drove in the back parking lot of the State Police office. "We have a project for all of you," Tony greeted the officers who were in the big back room. "You all know Hardin, and this is Brant Grayson. Some of you have met him."

Tony laid the map on the table and told everyone what they were looking for.

"His description doesn't ring a bell with me," Brant said. "I haven't been here long enough, and I don't know all those little back roads. Hardin, do you suppose it could be anywhere near where he shot Barney?"

"Well-l-l," Hardin considered. "That was about here. We went from Rivermount by the back road, not the highway, but it gets to the same place as where Colman said they turned off. That isn't as far away, though, as Colman sounded like they went. On a paved road for quite awhile. That'd be here, then a gravel road, maybe this one? What d'you think, guys?"

"Or it could be they went further and took this one," Tony said.

"What's going on here, map reading class?" a big voice boomed behind them.

"Hi, Burton," Tony said to the large trooper who had just arrived. "Come and look," and he explained what they wanted.

"Hell, I don't have to look," Burton said. "I know the place you're talking about. It's here," and he pointed to a spot on the map.

"You've been there?" Hardin asked. "You know the guy?"

"Yes and no, in that order. I've been there, but I don't know the owner."

"We've lucked out, friends," Hardin said. "Let's get down to planning this expedition. I'm assuming he's there. It looks like our best bet from what we know. I hope you can come with us, Burton? Let's figure out how many we need."

The troopers sat down around the big table with Hardin and Brant to decide who would go to the cabin and when. With Burton's help they planned to leave in order to arrive at the cabin area at dusk.

"We know the guy has at least two rifles," Hardin said, "and he's killed two people already. I don't want any of us hurt. There's no way to sneak up on the house since it's out in the open, but we can surround it though."

"Let's break for lunch and whatever else you need to do this afternoon, and we'll meet at this forest road here at six o'clock. It'll take us another hour to get there. That should be about right. This rain and cloud cover'll make the light better for us. You take care of the OSP end, Tony, and I'll do the sheriff's department. See you later."

"You want to come?" Hardin asked Brant as he drove back to the Justice Center in town.

"It's not what the doctor would order, but, yes, I don't want to miss it if this is the end of our hunt. I have a very large bone to pick with this guy. If Chuck can run me home, I'll rest this afternoon. Lisl will scold me, but I'll be bull-headed."

Hardin came by Campbell's house early in the evening to get Brant. Lisl wasn't there to complain, but Elaine indicated she thought Brant had a screw loose somewhere. Phil, however, would have been happy to go along if the car hadn't already been full.

Three pick-up trucks waited at the meeting place, two from the State Police and one from the sheriff's department. Burton and Tony led the way as the procession started into the forest with the rain continuing to drip. More than an hour later they jounced onto a muddy track and all stopped.

"It's less'n a mile," Burton told them. "I reckon we better go slow and quiet. We can stop part way and leave the cars and head into the bush on foot. You can maybe use the garage for cover to get up closer to the house. Once we got the place surrounded, then you can yell at him," he said to Hardin, "and see what happens."

"We want this perp alive," Hardin cautioned. "He can tell us a lot we don't know."

The cloud cover cast a dull gray light over the clearing when Hardin and Brant looked from the forest edge. The little creek babbling over the rocks made the only sound. Even the rain drops had shifted to a silent mist.

"Looks deader'n a doornail," Hardin whispered. "You think he's here or are we too late maybe?"

"Let's ease up to the garage," Brant said. "We can get there without being seen from the cabin."

"He's here," Brant said. "There's the car." The shape of a dark Toyota barely showed in the dim light.

"Okay," Hardin said. "Everyone's in place. Let's see what happens," and he raised his voice.

"Jerome Billings, come out with your hands up. This is the police. You are surrounded."

Silence. The rippling creek made the only reply.

"Come out, Billings," Hardin yelled again.

Still no sound.

"What d'you think?" Hardin turned to Brant.

"Looks strange," Brant whispered. "No smoke from the fireplace, no light, the door is unlatched. Fire a shot in the air, and see if it brings a response."

Hardin whispered his intention into his radio to alert the other officers, then fired his rifle. The noise echoed through the clearing.

No response.

"I'm going up to the porch," Hardin said. "You stay here. I'll get Tony or Burton to come too."

Brant watched in the darkening light as Hardin ran toward the cabin with Burton coming from the other direction. Hardin eased the door open while Burton peeked around the edge of the window.

"Stand down, men," Hardin yelled. "We're too late. He's dead."

Brant felt a huge sense of relief, but a flash of disappointment too. Deep inside him something elemental in his nature wanted to hunt the man down. He walked toward the cabin wondering who had beat him to it.

Tony came toward the cabin as the other officers emerged from their hiding places among the trees.

"Watch for foot tracks," he told them, "or car tracks. And put the tape round the whole clearing. I'll see who I can raise on the phone and get the process started."

Brant stepped carefully into the room. Jerome lay face down across the table. Hardin had found a lantern and lit it.

"Looks like a small caliber hand gun. Two bullets through the body from the front and one close up to the head. Whoever did it wanted to make sure."

Brant moved over to the body and touched it.

"Yesterday probably. He was a liability but to whom? Frank or Colman?"

"Couldn't have been Colman. He didn't get back until late last night. I'd say this happened more'n 24 hours ago."

Brant looked around. A couple of wooden chairs stood on either side of the table in the center of the room with a cellular phone lying at one end. To the left was the kitchen end with a sink and two cupboards. At the right end sat a single bed with a sleeping bag. Some clothes hung from nails in the wall. A nondescript dresser by the bed held whatever else Jerome had brought with him in clothes. Two rifles stood in the corner, a 30.06 and a Winchester 300 Magnum. On the floor by the dresser sat the pair of cobra skin cowboy boots Brant had seen before.

The ashes in the fireplace were cold. No footprints were wet or muddy except their own. A bowl and a glass in the sink could have been from either lunch or supper, maybe even breakfast. The coffee pot on the propane gas stove still had coffee in it.

Brant opened the refrigerator. It was well stocked.

"He was planning to stay awhile. Bacon, eggs, apples, potatoes. And a pan of left-over soup. The freezer is full too, bread, meat, juice." He opened one of the cupboards by the sink. Coffee, soup cans, tuna fish, peanut butter, pancake mix, a box of cereal. In the back Brant found a large, economy size bottle of bourbon.

"I'm guessing he'd just had lunch, soup and a peanut butter sandwich. There's peanut butter on this knife." Brant sniffed the glass. "And he had some bourbon to wash it down. The medical examiner can verify all that. We'll have to wait until daylight to check for tracks outside, but what I see in here confirms our estimate of the time – yesterday early afternoon before the rain hit here. If that lets Colman out, I can't think of anyone else besides Frank who might have known about this place and might have wanted to get rid of Jerome before he could talk to us."

Hardin and Tony stayed behind to wait for the crime scene crew while the rest of the officers headed back to town. They dropped Brant off at Campbells.

Lisl welcomed him and chided him at the same time.

"I'm so glad to see you, but you should never have gone out. Where have you been so late? You look tired. Come sit down."

"What happened?" Phil wanted to know. "Did you find the guy?"

"I have good news for everyone," Brant said as he eased himself into a comfortable chair. "Lisl and I can go home tomorrow, and we can all relax."

"You caught him," Lisl exclaimed. "Oh, I'm so glad and relieved. Is he in jail?"

"No, he's headed for the morgue."

"Oh."

"That's not how you wanted it, I'll bet," Phil said.

"No, we hoped to get information from him."

"I'll call Westons and Michaels," Elaine said. "They'll want to know too. We've all been worried," and she headed for the phone in the kitchen. In a few minutes she was back with the news that the foursome were on the way over even though it was late, and not to say anything until they got there because they didn't want to miss a word.

Saturday

Brant called Hardin next morning. Hardin sounded a little groggy.

"It took a large chunk out of the night to get things finished out there. I'll be going out again this morning to check around outside. Jerome is on his way to Portland to the Medical Examiner and an autopsy. We'll have to wait for the results of that to know for sure what time frame we're interested in. And then there's ballistics results for both rifles and for the gun that killed him. I called Colman Lewis this morning to tell him Jerome is dead. He sounded relieved. He wanted to know when he could leave the area – said he has work to do. I told him to stick around a few more days. I won't be able to hold him here much longer unless we have something to charge him with."

"Something will turn up. What about Frank? Has anyone talked to him yet?"

"Chuck is on his way there now."

"How about looking into Colman's business in California? Know anyone there who could be counted on to take an interest?"

"I'll have to think about that. Now that Jerome's out of the picture, I'm not sure we have enough evidence to get any kind of a warrant there."

"Here's a better idea. Why don't you try the customs department? They're guaranteed to be interested if it involves illegal imports. And Clyde Bennett at the lab in

Ashland can probably give you some help with the U.S. Fish and Wildlife people down there."

"That's a great idea. I'll talk to Tony about it since he's the one who took all that stuff down to the lab. I'll keep you posted. Where're you going to be?"

"That's what I called to tell you. Lisl and I are going to move back to our own homes and quit sponging off our friends."

"They loved having you and being part of the whole thing. You know that. Do you think it's safe to go home? You think Frank isn't a threat?"

"Frank was only involved at Jerome's behest. If he killed Jerome, it was only to save his own skin. I don't think he's interested in me any longer. There's nothing I could tell or do that the police don't already know about as far as he's concerned."

"I guess you're right; but still, be careful. Jerome killed two people and tried to get you, and his killer is still out there."

By the time Brant hung up the phone, Lisl had their suitcases packed and ready to move home. They said their thanks to Campbells and drove to Lisl's house.

"Come on in," she said. "Let's put a load in the washing machine and relax for a little while. It's been a hectic week to put it mildly. How are you feeling? You looked so tired last night."

"I'm lots better. It's been over a week now since the accident, and I think the bones are growing together. I'm not up to full speed yet, but life looks brighter. Are you going in to work?"

"For a little while. Why don't you come over for dinner. It's Saturday night, and we're free of worry so we can celebrate. I'll take you home now and pick you up late this afternoon. How's that?"

"Sounds good to me."

Brant busied himself tidying up his house. After a week away, it needed a little attention. He didn't think he was a neatnik, but it bugged him when he could see a layer of dust over everything.

Workmen had been in to repair the window and the kitchen woodwork. Done a nice job, Brant decided as he ran his hand over the patched wood. He'd been busy more than an hour when the phone rang. The noise in the quiet house startled him and made his heart pound.

How long would it take before he could react to a ringing phone without fear, he wondered as he went to answer it. It was only Hardin.

"Just thought you might like to know Tony left already for San Francisco. The customs people are delighted to have him come. They've had their eye on Lewis' business for some time, but hadn't ever managed to pin anything on him."

"Maybe working from that end will give us what we need. And another thing I thought about – see if Colman actually did arrive on that late commuter flight or if maybe he was on an earlier one. Then you can confirm with Esteban when he came back to the house."

"Will do."

Lisl came by at four o'clock. The rain from last night had stopped after washing the sky to a shining blue.

"Let's barbecue a couple of steaks. I have some potato salad. We'll have a summer meal with fresh strawberries for dessert.""

"That sounds super," Brant said "You beautiful ladies are spoiling me. I'm not used to the gourmet meals all of you have cooked up the past week."

They sat out on the back deck in the late afternoon sunshine and watched the golfers go by pursuing their little white balls down the fairway. A hawk soared lazily through the still air riding the warm updrafts.

"I can almost imagine none of this past week happened," Brant said. "It's so peaceful."

"I know just what you mean. It's been bad for you, and not just this week. Ever since we found the dead elk and that poor man on our hike. Now two more men are dead, and you were nearly killed. Jerome murdered the other two, but who killed him?"

Brant had steered away from Lewis' possible involvement. All he'd told his friends about Colman was his help in pin-pointing Jerome's cabin and his professed innocence about the elk hunt.

"That's our latest mystery. Hardin and Tony and Chuck and all the rest of the police are working on it. I'll leave it to them to finish."

"Good. You can go back to being retired again, and I'll be happy about that. I've come closer to murders since I met you than I ever had in my life, and I'll be glad never to see one again. And glad never to visit you in the hospital or go with you to the emergency room again."

Supper was over. Brant and Lisl, feeling well-fed and contented, watched the sun edge down toward the mountain peaks.

"You know," she said, "I think it would be nice if I called Colman and told him how sorry we all are about how this turned out. It must be dreadful for him to know the foreman he trusted turned out to be a murderer." She reached for the portable phone on the table.

Brant didn't see any need for her to call, but he didn't want to argue. It was too nice an evening.

"Buenas tardes, Esteban. May I speak to Senor Lewis, por favor?" - "He's not there? When do you expect him back?" - "He's gone to the airport?" Brant came out of his lethargy in a hurry.

"Ask him how long ago and which airport," he said to Lisl.

"How long ago did he leave?" Lisl asked. "Just a few minutes. And which airport? Farwell. Gracias, Esteban. Buenas noches."

"Come on, get your car." Brant grabbed Lisl's hand and headed for the garage. "No time to lose if we want to stop him."

"But why do we want to stop him, and we don't have any right to, do we?"

"Just come, and I'll tell you in the car."

"Now tell me what this is all about," Lisl said when they were in her car and on their way out of Rivermount.

"Colman shouldn't be leaving the area, and he knows it. Hardin told him just this morning to stay here at least a few more days until the police get the results of the autopsy and ballistics tests and that sort of thing."

"But what do those things have to do with Colman?" she asked as she sped up the highway.

"We haven't wanted to say anything definite until we are sure, but it looks very much as if Colman's business is involved in illegal trade items. And Jerome didn't kill himself so his killer is still at large."

"You don't think Colman killed him, surely?"

"Colman said he didn't get here until the last commuter flight which would be after Jerome was killed. Hardin is checking to see if perhaps he came in earlier than he said. He was also going to check with Esteban as to when Colman actually arrived at the ranch. It's just more than possible that's what caused Colman to decide to leave so suddenly."

"But shouldn't we be calling Hardin?"

"Yes, and I will as soon as we get to the airport. This is one time I wish I had a phone in the car. If he's going to Farwell's airport, it's because he's chartered a plane since there aren't any commercial flights from there. I don't want to lose a minute getting there."

Lisl drove as fast as she dared, but Brant wished he had flashing lights and a siren. The trip from Rivermount to the airport would normally take close to half an hour, but Lisl managed to shave a few minutes off. It would take Colman equally as long or longer from his ranch which meant that he couldn't be more than a few minutes ahead of them.

Brant jumped out of the car at the front entrance of the small terminal wincing as he forgot about bones not yet healed.

"Park and then come on in," he told her as he dashed for the door.

Through the back windows he could see a small plane warming up and Colman just going out the door toward it. Brant ran to the door and yelled. Colman turned. He had one hand in his pocket and a briefcase in the other.

"Where do you think you're going?" Brant shouted over the noise of the plane's engine.

"What business is it of yours?" Colman answered.

"You're part of a criminal investigation, and the police have told you not to leave the area."

"I'm not under arrest, and I'll go when and where I please. You're meddling in something that is not your affair. You should go back to being retired. It would suit you better."

Brant moved closer. The back of his mind told him he was in no condition to physically restrain Colman, but maybe he could deter him psychologically. He hadn't noticed in his dash through the terminal if anyone else was around.

"You're not going anywhere. Jerome wasn't running his poaching operation on his own, and you had the best motive of anyone for getting rid of him before he could spill the whole story."

"I'm getting on this plane, and you can't stop me. I'll be safely out of the country tonight."

Brant moved a step closer.

"Don't even think about trying to stop me." The menace in Colman's voice matched the gun in his hand as it came out of his pocket and pointed at Brant. This wasn't the first time a gun had ever been pointed at him, but his stomach turned over and his heart jumped just the same. Looking down the barrel of a gun can cause anyone's blood pressure to zoom up. A week ago he would never have suspected Colman of anything more nefarious than trying to steal Lisl away from him.

A flash of movement inside the building caught his eye. Lisl was at a telephone. If he could keep Colman talking long enough, the police would get here.

"You can run, but you can't get away. Your illegal empire will come crashing down on you. Those things we took from your house are just the tip of the iceberg."

"I don't know what you're talking about – my illegal empire," Colman sneered. "Your trolley is off the track. My business is entirely legitimate. I may sue you for libel."

"Where did Jerome get his cobra skin boots?"

"Oh, those," Colman laughed. "I brought them back one trip for him. I knew he'd like them. He had no sense of good taste when it came to his clothes."

"How many other little gifts have you smuggled in over the years. And how many elk trophy heads have gone out? Is that the gun you used to kill Jerome?"

"You are talking total nonsense. And don't come a step closer," as Brant edged nearer. "I'm leaving now."

Anger boiled up in Brant. "You thought you could make fools of the police with that tale about Jerome's cabin. You knew exactly where it was because you'd been there the day before. You knew if you gave us a good hint where he might be that we'd hunt 'til we found him. And your story about not getting here until late that night was just a story. You came in on an earlier flight, but you didn't get home until late. Plenty of time to get to Jerome's cabin and shoot him." Brant watched Colman's face to see if his guesses had hit home.

"You do rave on," Colman said with what seemed to Brant slightly less arrogance. "You really have slipped a cog, old man. No wonder you were nothing but a policeman all your life. I'm mystified what Lisl sees in you. And now I really must be going. Nice talking to you."

Brant had all he could do to keep himself from trying to tackle Colman. He knew the man was just trying to needle him into doing something rash that would give him an excuse to shoot at Brant. Hurry up, Hardin, Brant thought. How much longer can I keep him here?

Colman walked backward toward the plane keeping his gun pointed at Brant. He threw his briefcase in the open door and reached out his hand to pull himself on board, but the plane started to move at that moment. He was thrown off balance, fell against the fuselage and dropped the gun. In two quick steps Brant reached him and kicked his feet out from under him. As he fell, Colman reached for the gun on the asphalt, but a hand snatched it out of his grasp.

"Colman!" Lisl shouted, "how could you do this when we trusted you as a friend?"

"Silly bitch," Colman yelled back at her. Brant restrained himself with difficulty. He'd like to have bashed Colman's head against the pavement.

The noise of the plane engine stopped abruptly, and the pilot emerged. "Thought you needed some help," he said laconically. "I don't fly people with guns."

The noise of sirens approaching replaced the engine noise. Brant was surprised to see Lisl holding Colman's gun in a business-like fashion pointed directly at its owner. Colman rolled over and sat up.

"Don't move any further," Lisl ordered as she held the gun steady. Colman's jaw dropped in amazement. Brant wanted to hug her and laugh at the same time. He postponed his impulses when the flashing lights of the police cars lit the scene. Hardin came through the terminal as other deputies came around both ends of the building.

"On your feet, Lewis," he ordered. "You're under arrest."

"Lieutenant, you have this all wrong," Colman complained as he struggled upright. "These two assaulted me and held a gun on me as you can see. I want to file a complaint."

"You may do that when you get to the station if you so desire. Meanwhile you're still under arrest."

"On what grounds?"

"Suspicion of murder, fleeing to escape prosecution, dealing in illegal goods, probably a few more charges when we get it all together. Take him in, and read him his rights," he said to one of the deputies.

"You'll be hearing from my lawyer. False arrest, this is," Colman shouted as he was led away.

"Maybe I should take that gun now," Hardin said to Lisl. She still held it pointed at Colman's disappearing back.

"Oh, yes, of course, here," and she held her hand out to him looking thoroughly bemused. "I've never held a gun in my life before."

Hardin laughed. "You gave a very good impressions of knowing what it was for. Am I ever glad you got here before he had time to take off. How'd you know to come?"

"Lisl's the heroine. She decided to call Colman to say how sorry she was about Jerome's murder and all that, but we found out he had just left for this airport. I knew he must be planning to charter a plane."

"When I came in from parking the car," Lisl said, "I saw he was holding a gun pointed at Brant so I called you right away. I can't believe that nice man is definitely not a nice man."

They talked as they headed for the parking lot.

"I found out he came in on an earlier flight just like you thought," he said, "but Esteban said he didn't get to the ranch until late, the time he'd have been expected to arrive if he'd taken the late commuter. That gave him plenty of time to drive out to Jerome's cabin and kill him, and I expect this is the gun he used. When I found out all that, I had an idea he might decide to take off, but I wasn't in a hurry since there wasn't another commuter out until late. I didn't think he'd charter a plane here, because then he'd have had his car at the wrong airport. We were watching the main airport."

"I'm glad you came when you did," Brant said. "Who knows what Annie Oakley, here, might have done with that gun." He slipped his good arm around Lisl.

"Where're you gonna be tomorrow in case I want to bring you up to date? The way you bounce around from one house to another, I never know where to find you."

"I don't know. Where're we gonna be?" Brant asked Lisl.

"Let's have a pot luck picnic at your house with everyone – Westons and Michaels and Campbells. They'll all want to know what's happened. You're invited too if you'd like to come, Hardin."

"Thanks, I'll take a rain check. I think I'll be little busy tomorrow getting this mess all straightened out. I'll call you sometime to let you know what's going on."

CHAPTER TWENTY-SIX

Sunday Afternoon

Summer Sunday afternoon and the living is easy. The eight friends sat on the deck at Brant's house sipping tall, cold drinks. Amber lay under the table, totally relaxed, happy to be included in the party.

"Now tell us all about it," Caro said. "Am I hearing right that Colman is in jail for murder?"

"Yes, you heard right," Lisl said. "I wouldn't have believed it either except that I was there."

"How did you find out what he was up to?" Phil wanted to know.

"Hardin called just a little while ago. Tony Marcus from the Oregon State Police went to California yesterday. They went to Colman's business and to his warehouse, Tony and the customs agents. Tony said that warehouse looked like the one at the Forensic lab, crammed with every type of goods imaginable and mostly made from illegal kills all smuggled into the country along with his legitimate imports. Also the ballistics results showed it was his gun that killed Jerome. We found out he'd lied about when he flew here. He said it wasn't until after Jerome had been killed, but actually it was earlier – plenty early enough to have had time to do it."

"So he made most of his money illegally, huh," Jud said. "Too bad. He seemed like a great guy."

"At least we had the fun of seeing his gorgeous house and having that elegant dinner," Angie said. "I wonder what will happen to the ranch."

"He'll undoubtedly hire some high priced lawyers, and there'll be a long trial and appeals and all that stuff. It won't be settled for ages, I'll bet," Doc said.

The conversation drifted on to other subjects over dinner. Late in the evening after all the guests had gone except Lisl, she and Brant sat together watching the stars twinkle on as the sunset faded into dark.

Lisl took Brant's hand. Could it have been only a little over a week since Brant had been hurt? She hated the thought of hospital visits, and yet she was sure she wanted him to be a part of her life from now on. He brought her hand up to kiss it. She felt safe now with time stretching ahead of them as bright as the stars overhead.

"I'm glad it's finished, and I'm happy to be safe with you. I was so angry with Colman last night that I think I might actually have shot him if he'd tried anything funny. How could we have been so fooled by him?"

"Easy," Brant said. "Con men all seem credible or they wouldn't be successful. But enough of him and all his cohorts. I'm getting back to good health, and our life can go on from here with nothing but good things happening. You know what I'd like to do tomorrow?"

"What?"

"Let's go look for a new car for me."

"Oh, good, I love looking at new cars. What kind do you think you want?"

"I think it's time in my life for something more exciting than my usual dull sedan. How about a red convertible sports car?"